Fighting regret and grief over his wife's death, Joshua Campbell is sent to a resort in the Bahamas by his brothers as a way to recharge and unwind. All he expects to do is relax and maybe play a few games with his fellow vacationers. The last thing he wants is to hook up with anyone while memories of his late wife still haunt him.

Newly single Lauren Richardson's ex-husband's betrayal was enough to call an end to anything commitment-wise for a while. Relaxing on a tropical beach is a great way to rebuild her flagging confidence. She doesn't want any more ties, especially with a sexy Siksika man she runs into on a secluded part of the beach.

Joshua gives Lauren a fake name to hide his background, and a spark ignites that sets their libidos on fire. A few more encounters lead to a night of erotic pleasure, forging a bond that makes them wonder if their fun could go beyond their excitement in the sun. Tragedy strikes, ripping them apart, sending Joshua into a deeper sense of despair, and leaving Lauren wondering if she'll ever see the father of her child again.

Could Have Been
Copyright © 2024 V.J. Allison
ISBN: 978-1-4874-4165-4
Cover art by Martine Jardin

Published by eXtasy Books Inc

Look for us online at:
www.eXtasybooks.com

Could Have Been
The Feathered Tartan 4

By

V.J. Allison

DEDICATION

For Heather Tade, my best friend and twin sister soul, who gave me the original idea for Lauren and Joshua's story.

In memory of Adrien L. Naugler, who left this earth on September 8, 2021.
Fly with eagles, old friend.

PROLOGUE

Two Months Ago
Campbell Home, Bedford, Nova Scotia, Canada

The stench of tobacco burned Ewan Campbell's nostrils, the soft breeze carrying the smoke toward the back door. Mosquitoes buzzed around the bug zapper at the corner of the house. One hit it with a loud snap, echoing in the silence of the backyard.

His cousin Joshua sat in the Adirondack chair to the right, facing the swing set that was hiding in the shadows. He plopped a cigarette butt into the can on the glass table to his left, a hiss penetrating the air, pulled something out of his pocket and a moment later, the flare of a lighter flashed a moment before an ember appeared.

Ewan frowned. He hated cigarette smoke. It reeked worse than rotten seaweed, and always made him feel sick. He didn't want to inhale any of that shit, nor did he want Marti or the kids getting it into their lungs. Thankfully Joshua was only at the house during the daytime, and smoked outside, using an apple juice can as an ashtray.

He took three steps, flopped down on the matching chair beside Joshua, and put his can of iced tea on the wooden deck beside his feet. "Didn't you just put one out?" He leaned back in his chair, crossed his ankles, and shot his cousin a pointed frown to indicate his disgust.

Joshua narrowed his eyes in the shadows, and his jaw tightened. "I'm not in the house, and I'm using the can you

1

gave me." There was a lot of snark in his tone, enough that it made Ewan's eyebrows shoot up.

There was also a layer of hurt underneath the defensive attitude.

Ewan easily recognized it as the memories of Miranda hauling him into her office and rightfully giving him hell for his actions a long time ago. He used the same tone with her, until she pleaded with him to listen and offered the one thing he desperately needed — a helping hand, one he was going to offer Joshua, once his cousin let go of the defensive attitude and admitted he had more than one problem.

Ewan wondered if the guilt from not taking Sybil to the emergency room was eating Joshua from the inside out. Going by the way his cousin was chain-smoking, the way his hands were shaking, and how much he guzzled alcohol at Dana's wedding reception, Ewan guessed Joshua's internal hurricane of agony and remorse was driving him to the brink, making him more apt to smoke and be snippy with others.

Ewan would bet his entire savings that Joshua's self-loathing was overtaking his entire being, just like his had in the years after Marti left him.

He guessed Joshua's hate for himself was keeping him from moving forward, like his own had back then. It was like an open, festering wound that would continue to eat Joshua alive if he didn't snap out of it, soon.

"Fine. Get lung cancer. See if we care," he shot back, slapping a lot of disgust into his voice to hide the concern that was building in his chest.

Joshua glanced his way and dropped the half-smoked cigarette into the can, sending a plume of water vapor and a fizzle into the air.

Silence lapsed into the evening. Ewan let his cousin stew while he stole the occasional glance at the other man.

There were lines of exhaustion and agony on Joshua's

ashen face, his long black hair unkempt, stubble on his cheeks and chin, and his hands trembled every time he moved. His cheeks looked hollow, like he hadn't been eating properly, and his clothing hung off of him. It was a long way from the man who ran ten miles a day, every day, whether it was around the Campbell complex in Langdon, or on a treadmill during the cold and wet days.

Ewan inwardly cringed. He had seen the exact same thing in the mirror at one point. It hadn't made him stop punishing himself for everything, though. A person could continue to spiral downward if they wanted to, even if help was offered.

Concern rose higher in his chest. Joshua wasn't just his cousin. He loved the man like a brother. They were three years apart, but were closer than twins, or they had been, until Sybil's death a year ago. Once he let out his initial agony, Joshua had pulled away from Ewan and Dana, putting up walls topped with razor wire.

Having his cousin pull away from him hurt, and Ewan was sick of being rebuffed. Despite everything, it didn't stop him from wanting to help Joshua.

He could guess what was flowing through his cousin's mind. The urge to smash his head against a brick wall was there, but so was the need to stop the guilt and agony from burning their way into the brain, and to numb the torture, somehow—all to make it from one minute to the next.

Ewan wondered if the chain-smoking was part of Joshua's coping mechanism. His cousin had smoked for a few years, but quit when he started dating Sybil thirteen years ago. It wasn't surprising that Joshua's addiction to tobacco had reared its head again. Quitting nicotine was almost as bad as withdrawing from heroin, or so he'd heard. It was also easy to fall back upon in times of stress, like losing your soulmate forever.

Alcohol wasn't an easy thing to leave behind, either. Ewan

knew that firsthand. The first week or so after he stopped drinking was pure hell. He puked for three days, shook that entire time, and felt like he was being punched repeatedly from the inside out. The migraines had him in bed when he wasn't hugging the toilet or lying on the bathroom floor, wishing he would die.

A wave of sympathy for his cousin washed over him. If Joshua was already going down the dependences road with tobacco, it could spiral into something else. Ewan suspected Joshua was already drinking heavily, and if someone didn't try to help him, it wouldn't be a large leap to drugs like heroin or other opioids.

His worry over his cousin's well-being expanded, so much that he couldn't keep still in his chair. He let out a long sigh.

"They recruited you, didn't they?" Joshua's voice had a hint of *fuck you* overlying the agony he must have been feeling.

The porch light came on, penetrating the darkness surrounding them.

Ewan glanced at his cousin and shoved his glasses up on his nose. "Nope," he replied, keeping his voice neutral.

"Then why are you out here, instead of inside with your wife, kids and parents?"

Ewan easily heard the *fuck off and leave me alone* in Joshua's tone, but he ignored it. His cousin needed help, and he was the most qualified to give it.

But how could he explain that he knew exactly what was going through Joshua's head without completely coming clean about his own actions? Back then, he had done everything he could have done to keep his mind from going a mile a nanosecond — from sleeping with multiple women to drinking so much that he blacked out and didn't know how he landed in someone else's bed or how he got to work every day.

Another glance at Joshua's agony-filled, haggard features told Ewan how to approach the subject. "I'm here because worried about you." It was so hard to keep his anguish over his cousin's slide into hell out of his tone.

Ewan was terrified to the point of almost dragging Joshua to an Alcoholics Anonymous meeting by the scruff of his neck or slapping him silly.

Since violence wasn't the right way to get his point across, he took a deep breath to calm himself and give his cousin a chance to comprehend that not everyone was angry with him for being depressed.

That wasn't his diagnosis, but his wife's. He was grateful for Marti's insight and her whispers that someone in Joshua's shoes might not respond as well as he had when confronted. Sometimes a murmur was heard while a scream was ignored.

Joshua blinked. "What, no shitting on me for stinking up your yard or your house when I go inside?" He turned away to stare out at the night.

Ewan let out a sarcastic snort that echoed around the yard. "Everyone else did that for me, including Aunt Bertha and Uncle Darren."

He glanced at Joshua again, this time with a long sigh, and let his worry leak into his voice. "Talk to me, cousin. You've been a shit this entire week, and you were really bad at Dana's wedding. Yeah, you smiled and clapped, but it was easy to see the black cloud over your head, and how fast you were downing the booze at the reception. Get it out, and don't lie to me. You know I ain't afraid to knock you into next year."

God, he hated doing this, but he had to get Joshua to face his pain. To keep his nerves steady, Ewan scooped up the can of iced tea, cracked it open and took a huge swig while he waited for his words to sink into Joshua's brain.

Bafflement, annoyance, confusion and anger crossed his cousin's features. "I wasn't a shit, as you put it. I didn't feel like celebrating." He finished his smoke and plopped the used butt into the can with a hiss of water.

The urge to growl rose in Ewan's throat but he let out a louder scoff, conveying he didn't believe Joshua any more than he believed their grandfather was going to accept Dana's choice of life partner. "That's bullshit and you know it. Even Dana saw how upset you were. It was like her wedding reminded you of your own." He shifted in his seat, narrowed his eyes, and allowed a look of disappointment to cross his features. With a lot of sympathy in his voice, he intoned, "You didn't have to come. Dana and Avery would have understood."

Joshua scratched the back of his neck and brushed a tendril of his hair off of his cheek. "Dana's like my baby sister. I had to be here for her on her big day."

Ewan understood. Dana was the sister he'd always wanted but never had. Missing her wedding would have cut a hole into his heart. He was grateful she wanted him and Marti there, as witnesses on her side, same with his parents. They loved her like their own daughter.

Being a grey cloud and a shit for guzzling booze at the reception was a bigger offense, in Ewan's opinion. He let out a long sigh. "Three beers in five minutes said a lot to me." He took another gulp of the iced tea and set the can on the table between them. "Guilt and pain aren't easily controlled, I know, but I'm scared if you keep going down this path, you're going to land in rehab, or worse."

He met Joshua's gaze and saw the black circles under the man's eyes. "You can't sleep without the booze, right? You gotta have something to numb the pain, and it's the only thing that works."

Joshua's eyes went wide.

Ewan let the agony of being separated from Marti and how he'd tried deadening it with alcohol and women come to the surface again. It hurt so fucking much that tears burned his eyes and it felt like liquid nitrogen was being poured down his throat. His voice almost cracked as he said flatly, "I wound up in AA at Miranda's orders after Marti and I split. Drinking myself into a stupor was the only way I could function. If it wasn't for knocking myself out silly with it, I would have been banging my head against a wall, just so I didn't have to think, or feel, or remember her and what happened, let alone wonder why she'd ended it."

The knot in his throat threatened to choke him as he recalled her final words to him that fateful day, and the burning in his chest—that lasted for almost a decade before they reconciled—rose again. The agony of that time made his voice thicken, something he wouldn't have allowed to happen if they were in Alberta and around their family.

"I'm looking at you and seeing the exact same shit I saw when I looked in the mirror back then. I see another broken man who can't let go of his pain of losing the person he loved the most and is wondering why she left him behind." He cleared his throat and leaned forward in the chair, the clanking of his identification bracelet echoing around the yard. "It hurt. Like motherfucking *hell*. But I got through it. It took me a couple of years to break through losing Marti to get back on my feet, but I did it." He reached over and put his hand on Joshua's shoulder, feeling the tension in his stance. The man must have been in agony to be that stiff.

With a long sigh, Ewan cleared his throat again and continued, unable to keep a pleading note out of his tone. "I don't want you to kill yourself, Joshua. Please, don't let your grief overtake you like I let mine almost destroy me."

Joshua coughed and shook his head. "I didn't know you were boozing it up. I thought you were exhausted from not sleeping much." His voice was shaking, just a little.

Ewan hoped with his entire being that his cousin was hearing what he'd gone through and was understanding he needed help. "I was a borderline alcoholic back then. If Miranda hadn't whooped me in the ass and made me look at the mess I created after Marti broke up with me, I would have drunk myself to death after a while. She helped me get out of that fucking deep hole and back on track again."

He held out a hand to his cousin. "For fuck's sake, let me help you out of the hole. Josh, I don't want to lose you like I almost lost myself." He ground his teeth together, feeling the full brunt of helplessness, and like he was going to drown in the agony again.

Joshua cringed and took a deep breath. He groaned deep in his chest. "I can't do this. Not alone," he choked out.

Hearing the tears in his cousin's voice, Ewan couldn't keep the desperation and worry out of his own as he promised, "You won't be alone. I will be with you every single step of the way."

Joshua leaned forward, put his elbows on his knees and fisted his hands in his hair. Tears lined his voice as he growled, "I miss her. I miss her so fucking much, man."

Ewan tightened his grip on Joshua's shoulder, hanging on for dear life to the man he loved like a brother. "Stop holding it in, Josh. Let it out. Holding it all in is what's making you drink," he commanded softly, adding an offer of something he knew Joshua needed—hope, and help.

He was offering his shoulder to his cousin for support, one he hoped Joshua would take. Ewan wanted to give his cousin the chance that Miranda had given him a decade earlier, when he was at rock bottom, fighting for air, and barely functioning.

Joshua leaned toward his cousin and started to weep. "Help me," he choked out. "Please, Ewan. Help me get rid of this fucking agony that burns me every fucking day." He growled in torment and let out a keening wail of misery. He fisted his hand around the front of Ewan's shirt and dropped his head to his cousin's shoulder.

Relief surged through Ewan as he let his cousin cling to him, letting out his agony. "I'm here," he replied softly and closed his eyes. He tightened his arms around Joshua and let out a long breath.

The most important step toward Joshua's return to sobriety had been taken. It would be a long road, but Ewan was determined to be there with his cousin, the brother of his heart.

One step, one day at a time.

CHAPTER ONE

Sunrise Retreat
The Bahamas

Lauren Richardson stared out the window of her deluxe suite, her reflection showcasing her grin. All she could see was aquamarine ocean, sand, endless blue sky and lush greenery.

She couldn't believe this view was hers for an entire week. It looked so different from home, yet was familiar in some ways. Home didn't have palm trees, but the trees lining the cliffs of her favourite beach were always lush and green in the summer, creating a backdrop for one of the amazing natural wonders of the world.

There was a brochure for the resort on the table by her bed. She lifted it up and smiled. A glance at the activities at the hotel made her heart race with excitement. There were games like chess and checkers like any other resort, but the water sports like polo and volleyball interested her more, as did the salsa dancing lessons, the scuba diving classes, and the snorkelling. There were evening shows by a few well-known singers who resided at the resort full time, and a few other, more interesting performances, like a magic act, and plays for all ages. There were two adults-only bars, but otherwise, the Sunrise Retreat was children-friendly. There were a lot of activities aimed at families, like a wave pool, waterslides, a children's theatre, and an alcohol-free nightclub for everyone twelve years old and older. There were many fun things to do and places to explore.

Lauren tapped her fingernails on the end table as she considered her options. Thoughts of laying on the white sand, soaking up the sun and just relaxing were just what she needed after finding her soon-to-be ex-husband Dorian in bed with her former best friend Mallory.

The double betrayal was enough for her parents to decide she needed a vacation, away from the dealership, and a *long* way from the loser and his new toy. They paid for her trip—it was an all-inclusive deal, thanks to a friend of her dad's in the travel industry.

So far, it was amazing, and a surge of gratitude for her parents rose in her chest. This was the first time she had nothing to do other than relax and pretend work didn't exist in more than a year.

She flipped her curls over a shoulder and sighed. Another glance outside had her gaze lingering on the beach. Sunbathing sounded like fun, even if she had to soak herself in sunblock.

With a giggle, she grabbed her bikini and got ready to have some fun on the shore.

Just a little while later she was walking along the sand, her large yellow tote over her shoulder. The beach itself wasn't overly crowded, just a few people here and there, either in family groups, pairs, or, like her, singles. Some were wearing bathing gear, others were in cover-ups and some were wearing shorts and t-shirts, with or without sandals or shoes. A few children dug into the sand, having fun, while others jumped in the surf, giggling and cheering happily. A few people nodded and smiled at her as she walked by them, one lady that looked to be about her grandmother's age said a friendly hello, and some waved at her. She waved back in return.

The sounds of the surf mixed with the call of the seagulls,

and happy chattering with the occasional excited squeal from a younger person rang in her ears as she trotted along, happy to be away from the burdens of real life for a while.

Although Lauren knew she'd want company later, she needed some downtime by herself, away from others. She glanced around and saw some craggy rocks on the east end of the beach. Hoping no one else had claimed that spot, she skipped toward it.

Lauren smiled when she saw that the other side of the small cliff was deserted. She spread out her blanket, plopped down on it, kicked off her flip-flops, and set her bag down beside her.

The ocean was a deeper blue than the sky above it, and they almost blended together at the horizon. At least one type of gull flew overhead, squawking, and some rode the waves further out. The smell of the Atlantic whirled around her, its briny and sandy scent intoxicating and rejuvenating.

It was so refreshing to be away from home, away from the prying eyes of her family, her work, and everything else. Lauren felt all of her inhibitions sliding away with the waning tide, and a sense of peace overtook her.

She slathered on tons of sunblock—being a redhead was a curse sometimes—and took a deep breath. The scent of the sea seemed to be magnified, so greatly that she could almost see the tides along the Fundy shore in her mind as she closed her eyes and let out a long breath.

Feeling a bit drowsy after her flight and the stress of the last few weeks, Lauren lay back on her blanket, using her bag as a pillow. Content for the first time since she caught her ex's lies, she let herself drift, pretending she was at sea.

Slumber soon overtook her.

Joshua felt like he was in a comfortable bath with a view.

Tropical fish swam past him, and all of the amazing creatures along the seabed were fascinating. The ocean was so clear it was easy to see to the bottom, even in twenty feet of water.

Among the lionfish, which was an invasive species according to the snorkelling brochure, he saw some beautifully coloured coral which he avoided, a lot of types of blue fish, and some kind of stingray—black with white dots and a long stinger—gliding along the bottom of the sea. The view from the surface of the crystal-clear water had been breathtaking, making him wish he had opted to try scuba diving instead of snorkelling. Maybe next time.

He lifted his head out of the water, took the snorkel out of his mouth, and shook his head, letting his braided hair flip over his shoulder. Although he loved the view and swimming along, he still tired easily and decided it was time to return to the beach.

He waded ashore not far from a group of ragged rocks and saw he was a ways east of his original starting point. He could see the snorkelling and kayak rental area a short walk from his position. Making his way onto the beach, he slipped his goggles, which held the snorkel in a loop on its strap, around his wrist so he wouldn't lose them. He then removed the flippers, sliding them around his other wrist, and started ambling toward the booth.

He walked around the corner of the rocks and saw a blue blanket with a yellow beach bag sitting upon it. Someone lay on the blanket, a woman, going by shape of the face. He could make out delicate features and an abundance of curly red hair from ten feet away.

Her eyes were closed, but Joshua could almost bet she had green or brown eyes, which were typical for redheads. Her hair looked like it was a natural colour—he couldn't see roots or anything else related to colouring it. A straight, medium-sized nose covered in a smattering of freckles led down to full lips in a natural rose-petal pink, and her high cheekbones had a pink tinge to them. Her right hand lay under head, and her left one slid behind her back.

He couldn't keep his gaze from traveling down her body, toward her chest. The bra part of her bikini must have gotten stuck under her at some point and shifted to the side, because her breasts were on replete display. A warning bell went off in his head that he should make a noise—any noise—and look away, but his gaze wandered back to her as if of its own free will.

Porcelain skin gleamed softly in the sunshine. Full breasts with pale pink nipples teased the air as she breathed. A flat stomach with a blue belly button ring winked at him. A blue bikini bottom protected her from being fully exposed to him or anyone else on that part of the beach.

Without thinking, Joshua kept moving his gaze down her body. Long, slim thighs led downward to her feet, with dainty toes painted a bright sapphire.

This woman, whoever she was, was beautifully flawless, and he suspected she'd be just as gorgeous covered up as she was with her breasts exposed to the air. He loved the female form, and seeing it in almost-perfect condition made him freeze instead of moving along, or shifting his eyes away from her.

He prompted himself to keep going, although the urge to linger and behold her beauty for a few more minutes rang in his mind.

A child dashing into the water to his right was a reminder that they were on a family-friendly beach and that he shouldn't have been looking at the woman's accidental nakedness snapped Joshua back to reality. He shook his head and took a deep breath, then focused his gaze upon the sand in front of his bare feet. Counting shells as he walked was a good distraction, and a way to keep his eyes off of the most delectable-looking female he had seen since his wife died.

He flipped his braided hair over his shoulder again and started marching, never looking to his left.

A seagull squawked overhead, making him jump.

A gasp to his left suggested the woman had just woken up. He risked a glance at her, and with relief, saw she had covered herself with a towel.

"Sorry, just passing through," he said with a wave and gave her a charming smile.

"It's okay," her voice was a soft contralto. "I must have fallen asleep. I should head back to the hotel anyway."

He turned his head toward her. She was smiling, her cheeks almost as red as the cloud of hair framing her face. She had slipped on a t-shirt, wrapped the towel around her waist, and tucked a strand of her hair behind an ear.

Her eyes were a brilliant blue, almost the same colour as the ocean.

His mental prediction had been almost right. She was even more beautiful while awake, and her body covered.

A weird jolt zinged up his spine. That azure gaze made her seem vulnerable, almost innocent, and it sent an odd emotion through him.

It was like she needed protection and he was her defender.

Joshua blinked and shook it off. With a nod, he held up the snorkel gear. "I'm on my way back to the booth."

She smiled, showing off her straight teeth. "How is the snorkelling?"

He shrugged. "It's pretty under the water. You'll have to try it. It's worth the effort just to see the coral."

She hugged her shirt closer to her. "Thank you. Have fun."

He smiled with a wave. "You, too."

Keeping his focus on the sand, Joshua let out a long sigh, puzzled at the encounter. After passing another set of rocks, he glanced over his shoulder. He couldn't see her, but he suspected she was straightening out her bikini top, and fast, just in case someone else came along that part of the beach. It would be highly embarrassing for her to have another wardrobe malfunction.

The thought of offering to keep her company briefly crossed his mind, but it was nixed as soon as he thought it. He was there as part of his therapy, to help him relax in a spot that didn't remind him of Sybil. He wasn't there to play around with other women.

He sighed and kept walking. He had no room in his life for a woman.

Sybil was the love of his life, and he wasn't going to dishonour her by fucking around with another one, not this soon.

CHAPTER TWO

Two days later
South Cabana Bar, Christmas Theme Night

Joshua leaned against the bar by the south pool, surveying the scene. He took a long sip of his carbonated water, the tingle of the fizz and the sourness of the lemon on his tongue.

The beat of a Christmas carol turned dance tune shook the floor, a catchy song that had his foot tapping. Lights flashed in the darkness, and a full moon started to rise over the beach. Dancers filled the floor, moving to the music, sweat glistening off their skin, some moulded together like two halves of one body. The smells of perspiration, perfume, booze, tobacco, and marijuana smoke almost masked the scent of lemon wafting from his glass as he held it to his lips.

He took a long gulp of his drink and wondered what had possessed him to visit one of the adults-only bars that night. The plague of booze still distantly called to him, and seeing all of the amazing beauty in tropical waters made him long for Sybil.

Melatonin wouldn't help his troubled sleep that night. Neither would hanging around an area that was so loud it made the floor shake.

With a long quiet sigh, Joshua plopped his now-empty glass on the bar and pushed himself away from it.

Just outside of the bar, in the crowd, someone hit his side, and he automatically reached out to hold them steady.

Soft, silky skin touched his fingers, and a cloud of strawberry-blonde curls hit his face, sending a whiff of something soft and feminine into his nose.

"Whoops, sorry!" The woman in his arms turned her head to look up at him. Her smile instantly turned sheepish as her azure gaze met his. "Oh. Hi there." She saluted him with her drink, a blue concoction in a tall glass.

Joshua grinned. It was the gorgeous redhead from the beach. He glanced down and with an inward sigh of relief, noted she was wearing a strapless crimson dress that hugged every luscious curve to her knees, with matching high-heeled sandals. Her lips were painted in bright red lipstick, and her eyes were outlined in brown liner, with lash extensions. Not many redheads could pull off a crimson dress, especially one that tight, but she did, beautifully.

She tucked a curl behind her ear and the pink on her cheekbones highlighted her runway-worthy looks. A long, gold chandelier earring winked at him for a moment.

He smiled at her kindly, feeling an unknown emotion rise in his gut. "No problem." He dropped his hands. "Did you get snorkelling?"

The redhead's eyes went wide and she giggled. "Not yet, maybe tomorrow." She stared up at him with a bigger smile. Her gaze moved downwards before meeting his again. "Want to join me?"

Joshua blinked. As gorgeous as this woman was, he didn't want companionship, only relaxation. He averted his gaze and scratched the top of his left forearm. "Uh . . . "

Her blue eyes turned cloudy and her smile faded. "You're not interested in women."

He shook his head. "It's not that, it's—"

She patted his arm. "Don't worry about it. You're a gorgeous man, and I thought since you recognized me in something other than my bikini, I thought it meant you wanted some company."

Fire creeped along his cheeks. He was used to attention from men and women, but never had anyone outside of his late wife been so blatantly honest with him about how they liked his looks. "Thank you," he mumbled and shoved his hands into his pants pockets with an awkward shuffle of his deck shoes on the stone walkway, unsure of how to respond other than gratitude.

She gave him a smile that seemed to light up her face, bringing the smattering of freckles along her cheeks into sharper focus. "If you were interested, I'd ask you to go salsa dancing with me." She flipped her hair over her left shoulder with a hand, the bright lights along the path catching the sparkle of stones set in a ring on her middle finger. She wasn't wearing a wedding band, but he knew that sometimes married people liked to pretend otherwise, so they could mess around. It was common in his parents' circuit as well as his own generation, although most of his attached cousins and siblings adored their spouses and didn't play games.

Unconsciously, he fisted his left hand and the quiet bite of his wedding ring dug into his fingers, a sharp reminder that he was only there to relax and recharge his drained batteries. He smiled at her and sighed. "Honestly, I swam all day and it's starting to catch up with me. I didn't realize it until a few minutes ago." It wasn't a lie. He hadn't been able to sleep properly in over a year, not since that fateful night that he lost his beloved.

She nodded with a slow blink, her eyelash extensions creating a smudged crescent on her cheeks for a second. "I understand. I'm still feeling a bit jet lagged myself." With a shrug, she took a sip of her drink and smiled again. Her lipstick left a red ring around the blue straw, creating a splash of crimson. "Get some rest. Maybe we'll run into each other again."

Her tone suggested she wouldn't mind having his company at some point. Whatever. He wasn't there for companionship, even with a woman with her striking looks.

Then why did his stomach churn at the thought of rejecting her invitation? His brow furrowed for an instant, but he relaxed it at the sight of her mouth drooping. The resort wasn't that big, not like a cruise ship. They'd probably see each other in passing now and then over the course of his time there, and seeing a familiar face wasn't unappealing to him. Maybe making a friend wouldn't be so bad.

He smiled. "I wouldn't mind."

Her grin in return seemed to light up the area brighter than the noon day sun. She switched her drink to her left hand and held out her right one, the silver bracelet on its wrist jangling in the warm air. "I'm Lauren." Her fingernails were painted a soft blue, the same as her toenails.

Dimly remembering Collin's instructions not to give away his identity to protect the family—which Joshua thought was dumb; who in their right minds cared about the fucking Campbells down here—he took her hand, shook it and nodded. "Davidson," he replied. His room was listed as Davidson Harper, his middle name and his Grandmother Iris' maiden name. Without thinking, he lifted her hand to his lips and kissed the back of it, a gesture from long ago.

Lauren's eyes widened, and pink spread across her cheeks. "That's the first time any man has kissed my hand." She blinked a few times and cocked her head to her right. "That is one weird name."

He grinned. "How so?"

She chuckled and took a sip of her drink via the straw. "Your parents named you after a motorcycle brand. Do they love riding motorbikes that much?"

Joshua cringed and shook his head with a sigh. Sybil had said the same thing to him when she found out his middle name. He scratched the back of his neck and cracked his jaw. "Uh, no, they don't like riding motorcycles. It's an old family name, it was my great-great grandmother's maiden name."

She nodded and clicked her tongue. "And they wanted to keep the family names within the family, right? My family does the same thing. My brother's name is Leroy, which was our great-uncle's name. I have no clue why my parents insisted on calling him that. Uncle Leroy was an asshole." She rolled her eyes with a snort.

Laughter bubbled in his chest. "Maybe they liked the name?"

Her eyes widened and she shuddered with a frown. "God, I hope not. I would never say this to my brother, but the name is hideous. I call him Lee, I'm the only one allowed to do that." There was a mischievous twinkle in her eyes, one that made Joshua realize this one had a great sense of humour and wasn't afraid of kidding around when the need hit her.

"I don't like that name either," he admitted. A glance back at the bar showed it was filling up fast, and another one at his watch showed it was past eleven Atlantic Time. No wonder he was tired. He had been up since before dawn, unable to sleep after dreaming of his lost wife.

A wave of sadness flooded his soul again, making his heart scream in agony. Keeping his left hand in his pocket, he rubbed the palm of his right one across his cheek and chin as he tried shoving the pain away.

A soft touch on his left forearm eased the flood of agony. "Is everything okay? You looked sad for a moment." Lauren blinked up at him with concern in her irises and her lips parted in worry.

He gave her a dejected smile and patted her hand with his free one. "I'm okay, thanks." With a glance at their linked fingers, he pulled his hand away and let out another long sigh. "Maybe I'll tell you about it sometime."

She nodded and winked up at him. "Sure." She looked toward the dance floor.

Joshua followed her gaze and saw someone waving at them.

She waved back with a grin and turned back to him. "I'd better get going. I met some people on the same floor as I'm on, and they invited me to hang out with them this evening." She fluttered her eyelashes at him a few times. "You are welcome to tag along, if you want." There was a hopeful note in her voice.

It was tempting, considering how comfortable he felt around Lauren, but at the same time, Joshua didn't feel like socializing with anyone else that evening. If it had been just her, he'd consider it. She was sweet, witty, seemed to have a bit of an evil side that he found attractive, and she was drop-dead gorgeous. Anyone would have been lucky to have her companionship.

With a long sigh of regret, he shook his head. "Another time?"

She gave him a bright smile, showing her straight teeth. "Sure, I'd love that. How's about I look for you at breakfast? You normally eat at the buffet, right?" One long fingernail traced down his arm, sending a shiver of something down his spine.

He mentally shook it off and nodded with one of his lop-sided grins, pleased that she remembered seeing him, although he didn't recall seeing her there. He had probably been too busy reading the newspaper or had his nose in an e-book on his phone. "You have a great memory. Sure, why not? I'd like that." He lifted her hand and kissed the back of it again, caught up in her sunshine mood. He lowered it with a wave. "Until tomorrow, sweet Lauren."

She blew him a kiss and giggled. "See you later, David." With a glance over her shoulder at him, she waved and walked toward her friends, who were beckoning her to join them.

With a long sigh, partially regretting his decision to go back to his room, Joshua shoved his hands into his pockets and turned to walk away.

Lauren was a lovely person, and she would have made a great companion for the evening, but she wasn't the one he wanted.

He wanted Sybil, and she no longer existed outside of the family's memory.

With a soft growl of agony, Joshua knew he wouldn't sleep that night.

CHAPTER THREE

Lauren grumbled to herself as she strode into the lobby the following morning, her flowing baby-blue dress flittering around her sandaled feet, a woven white sunhat on her head, and her beach bag over her shoulder. Whatever had possessed her to ask David to join her at the bar, and then breakfast? Sure, the man was good-looking and seemed sweet, but she didn't want a man at the moment—not even for some quick, hot sex.

She paused at the archway to the buffet and sighed when the reason why she asked him to tag along hit her.

There was a deep sorrow in the man's gaze despite the lopsided grin and the way he had kissed her hand. His entire soul seemed to be entrenched in torment, from what, she didn't know.

If she was smart, she'd duck out and run before she could find out. Men who were that deep in sorrow might not want to be cheered up.

However, Lauren wasn't one to turn tail and walk away from someone who was suffering. She was always the first one to offer someone a helping hand and a shoulder to cry on. If they didn't take it, that was their choice. She knew sometimes all a person needed was a listening ear and a kind smile to feel better.

She wanted to help David feel human again—even if it was as a friend. No one should have been suffering that level of pain she saw in his gaze.

"Leave it to me to try saving another lost soul," she muttered under her breath with a shake of her head, hoping that he'd forgotten about her impulsive agreement. With a long sigh, Lauren took a step into the buffet area next to the pool on the south side of the resort.

The sounds of laughter and water splashing hit her ears. She smiled towards the children playing in the pool, and the scent of chlorine wafted around her, along with the aromas of strong coffee, tea, and bananas. A glance towards the buffet on the right showed platters holding a variety of fruits ranging from strawberries to pineapples, papayas to mangos, and a few she couldn't identify were laid out next to containers of ice holding single-serving-sized yogurt and juice, along with condiments for coffee and tea, and urns holding hot drinks.

A few workers of various nationalities including Americans wearing the resort's logo on blue polo shirts were either continually checking the temperature of the fruits and other items or helping people get servings of their chosen foods. A male server with blond hair helped a child get a glass of juice from one of the dispensers, while one with dark hair and a big gentle smile handed a mug to a woman with long brown hair. The buffet wasn't as full as it was yesterday, but it was starting to fill up, fast, going by the amount of people walking past her toward the spread of food.

A movement a few feet off to the left made her smile. She instantly recognized the waist-length black hair tied back in a low ponytail with a leather band. He sat with his back to her, his broad shoulders covered in a white shirt that contrasted with his tan skin and dark hair.

He lifted a mug with his right hand, and the soft gleam of gold from a chained bracelet winked at her in the sunlight. A smattering of dark hair covered his forearm, highlighting the muscles moving beneath his skin. He set the cup down and moved his head to the left, then slowly toward the right, as if he was looking for something, or someone.

So maybe the handsome and sad David was waiting for her after all. She took a deep breath and took the three steps to his table, deliberately brushing his arm as she walked past him.

He glanced up and smiled when his eyes met hers, crinkles forming at the corners, the left side of his smile slightly higher than the right, showcasing his straight, white teeth. "Morning," he said, his low voice almost a rumble compared to the chatter around them. He rose to his feet and took her hand in his, lifting it to place a kiss on the back of it.

With a tingle low in her gut, Lauren gave him a smile in return and felt her cheeks warming up. No matter what went down between them—friendship or just having a breakfast together—she knew she'd always associate the gallant gesture and lopsided grins with David.

"Hi," she said breathily and gave his fingers a gentle squeeze, feeling a soft pressure in return. His fingers felt a bit calloused, like he worked with his hands. It sent a shiver deep into her core and a tremor up her spine. She was close enough to him to smell something spicy, like aftershave or cologne, and to feel his forearm brush her elbow when he lifted her hand to kiss it again.

"You look lovely," he said as he let go of her hand and gestured to the chair across from his.

When she went to pull it out, David reached around her and gently dragged it out with a smile.

Unused to having a man be that chivalrous toward her, she blinked up at him for a moment before hesitantly sitting down. As David walked back to his own chair, barely two feet in front of her across the white metal table, a few things hit her about Dorian. Her scheming ex had never held out a chair or even opened a door for her in the ten years they were together, not even when they first started dating.

She wasn't even dating David, and he'd been kinder to her

in the last three days than Dorian had been to her in their entire time together.

He eased his lanky frame down and leaned forward to pick up his mug. He lifted it to his lips and took a sip.

Seeing his Adam's apple bob up and down as he swallowed made another tremor slide deep into her core.

He lowered the mug and smiled at her. "I didn't think you'd show up this morning. I thought we were talking about another day."

Lauren felt her cheeks warming up, and it felt like she was blushing so much that it hid her freckles. "I must have gotten my wires crossed," she replied and fiddled with the spoon by her right hand, on top of the linen napkin beside the white plate they used at this resort.

"If you did, that's fine with me. I'm happy to see you." A look of confusion flashed across his face, then disappeared. "I hope you don't mind, but I already hit the coffee pot. I always have one before I have breakfast." He saluted her with the mug.

Elation ran through her chest when she realized he was glad to see her and have her company. It was another odd feeling, one she locked away to digest at a later time. This morning was about enjoying the company of a handsome well-mannered gentleman, not trying to figure out why she felt so happy to be in his presence.

"I'd kill for a coffee," she admitted, the smell of the brew making her soul sigh—her one bad habit, other than picking the wrong men. She set her beach bag on the floor to her right, removed her hat and put it on the bag as she started to push her chair back.

David immediately rose to his feet with a wave of his hand. "Stay put. I'll get you a cup. What do you take?" He picked up his own mug and grinned at her.

Oh my. A shiver of *something* zoomed up Lauren's spine.

She stared up at him, dumbfounded for a moment as she tried comprehending his manners, and how different he was from most men, other than her dad. Her jaw fell slack for a moment, then she tightened it, making her teeth clack together. "Um, cream and sugar?"

David's low chuckle echoed in her ears, sending another wave of something up her back. "Are you sure about that?" There was a teasing note in his flat-accented tone, and a twinkle in his deep brown eyes.

Heat burned her cheeks again. With a sigh, she nodded and put her hand over her mouth.

He chortled softly with a shake of his head. "One coffee with cream and sugar coming right up." Another snort, and he started walking toward the buffet.

Lauren's gaze followed him as he walked away from their table, a soft exhale blowing out between her lips. The short-sleeved shirt allowed his tan skin to show through it a bit, and it moulded to his broad shoulders perfectly, although it looked a little loose for him around his ribcage and back. Loose navy pants rolled up at the ankle and held with a black leather belt seemed to hang off of his legs but were tight enough around his butt to show it off a bit. Brown deck shoes without socks highlighted his ankles, visible between the cuffs of his trousers and shoes.

Dimly, she wondered if his skin was tan under his clothing as well, or if he had white patches under the trunks she'd seen him in the other day. God, he was handsome, even if he was on the thin side.

With a shake of her head, she shoved that thought away. *What was she thinking?* They had talked twice before that morning, and once while she was nearly naked in a bikini. It wasn't like they were going to be dating or anything.

Still, she couldn't seem to keep her eyes off his ass as he navigated toward the coffee urns and grabbed a fresh mug for her on the way.

He turned, and she ducked her head so he wouldn't catch her staring at him. With a grumble under her breath, Lauren forced herself to turn away and stare at her placemat.

"Here you go," David's voice rumbled in her ear, and a full mug appeared in her vision a moment later. The intoxicating scent of fresh coffee hit her nose, and she inhaled deeply.

"Thank you," she murmured with a smile.

He sat down across from her and lifted his own mug with both hands. "I hope it tastes okay. I wasn't sure how much sugar you take."

Lauren lifted the mug to her lips and took a sip. It wasn't as sweet as she normally took it, but it still tasted like heaven. "It's perfect," she replied, setting the cup down with a smile.

A smile that instantly faded when she noticed the soft gleam of gold on his left hand, the ring finger. Another wink of gold showed it was a plain band.

Shit. Of course a sweet guy like him would be married. It made sense.

Then why was he paying attention to her? Was he hoping for a fling? Well, he wasn't getting one with her. Having fun with a man was one thing, but encroaching on another person's territory was another. She didn't care if they had an open marriage or not, attached people were off-limits in her book. He could find someone else to play with, she wasn't having any of that.

With a small growl of annoyance, she reached down, grabbed her hat and slapped it on her head. "Sorry, I should go," she muttered and started pushing her chair back. Anger, disappointment and disgust hit her tongue, causing a sickly metallic taste in her mouth.

David's eyes widened and the corners of his mouth turned downwards. "What?" He blinked at her a few times and his left eyebrow rose a few notches.

Not one to hold the truth back when she was irritated, Lauren gestured to his hands and hissed, "I don't believe in stepping into another person's territory."

He blinked again and his head twitched backwards for a moment. "Territory?"

His confusion seemed genuine, as if he had forgotten to remove the offending wedding band, but that didn't stamp down her annoyance. "I don't mess around with married men, even if it's for coffee," she snapped softly.

His shoulders drooped and his face lost a lot of its colour as he slowly lowered his mug. Sorrow etched his features, and a long, soft sigh escaped his lips. His eyes darkened, and Lauren swore she saw tears forming in those deep brown depths.

David fisted his left hand and let out something akin to a growl of torment. "I was," he whispered. "But not now."

Distrust of his words made Lauren balk at his soft reply, but sympathy for his seemingly genuine distress slowed down her motions. Her bag remained on the floor and she leaned forward. "What happened?" If she found out later on that this was a farce and he was a brilliant actor, she'll rip his lungs out . . .

He shook his head, and his left fist connected the palm of his right hand with a soft slap. "She died a little over a year ago."

Compassion started rising in her gut, drowning out the warning bells ringing in her head. Warily, however, she asked, "What happened?"

His entire body seemed to go rigid, and he shifted in his chair, cricking his neck stiffly. His jaw tightened, and both hands fisted on the table. He glanced at his left hand, his lips curling as if he was holding back a flood of agony. Then he mumbled flatly, "Brain aneurysm. She had a headache for a few days and chalked it up to a migraine. She died three days after it started."

He squeezed his eyes shut for a moment, and a look of raw, deep, torture flashed across his features. He took a deep breath and let it out slowly. "I woke up that morning and found her in the bathroom, on the floor. She wasn't breathing. I tried to find a pulse, but couldn't. I don't remember much after that." His voice sounded distant, like he was still in shock over losing his wife.

His next words were almost lost in the chatter and other people enjoying a meal swirling around them. "I'd tried getting her to go to the hospital a few times, but she refused to go. She hated places like that. She even told me she'd rather die than go to an emergency room." He cleared his throat and rubbed the back of his right hand along his taunt jaw. "Guess she got her wish, eh?"

Lauren's red alert bells went silent as his words sank into her brain. Either this guy was an award-winning actor, or his words were true. His actions suggested true torture, and as her gaze met his, she spotted a deep, unending suffering. Understanding rose in her stomach, and her throat started to close.

To lose someone you adored in such a shocking and sudden way would have hurt—a lot. If she cared about a man that much, Lauren knew that losing him to death that suddenly would kill her—mentally and in every other way.

Seeing the gentleman before her almost writhing in his torment and possible guilt sent her sinking back into her chair, her body relaxing. She leaned forward, covered his fisted hand with hers, and whispered, "Holy shit. My god, David. I'm so sorry."

He blinked repeatedly, moved his gaze from hers, and let out a long sigh. Awkwardly he pulled his hands back and took a deep breath. "Thank you," he whispered and stretched his neck.

"You loved her, didn't you?" Compassion rose in her

throat. *That poor man, how he must have suffered.*

David glanced at his wedding band with his lips down-turned and nodded. "Very much," he murmured, barely audible over the noise around them. He let out a long sigh and lifted his coffee mug to his lips but didn't drink any of it.

An uneasy silence fell between them, causing the people in the pool and the chatter around them to echo louder in Lauren's ears. His gaze drifted toward the pool, but she suspected he wasn't seeing anything around him. She took a sip of her coffee, letting him gather his thoughts, glancing at him from under her lashes from time to time.

A man carrying a smiling baby walked past them, and something crossed David's features for a split second before he took a deep breath and squared his shoulders. He cleared his throat, and a heartbeat later, his face turned impassive.

It puzzled her. Why did he suddenly freeze his face into a mask? Was he worried that she'd think less of him if he showed his emotions?

Her questions faded when she heard him speak.

"Sorry, what was that?" she asked, pretending she didn't hear him over the din in the buffet area.

Across the table, her gaze met his. The left corner of his lips curled up slightly, as if he was amused. "I asked what you wanted for breakfast." This time, he took a long sip out of his mug, his dark eyes twinkling.

Baffled that he could switch his sorrow on and off like a light switch, Lauren narrowed her gaze at him. Either the man was faking, or he had decided to enjoy the day, and not wreck it with his pain.

Her gut said he wasn't faking it. Fake pain did not show in a person's gaze, even if they were an award-winning actor, and his eyes were full of agony, even when he seemed amused.

She let go of her suspicions and relaxed, still a bit thrown off by his chivalry. With a smile, she shook her head. "Thanks, but I'm okay. You get yours, then I'll get mine." She was used to being independent, not being doted on, even in friendship.

The right corner of his mouth slid upwards a notch, and he chuckled. "I'm not going up first. I'm only going now if you come with me." He stood and held out a hand to her. "Come on."

Lauren glanced at his right hand, then his face. His left eyebrow rose a hint, and he winked at her. On a whim, she tossed out, "Only if you go salsa dancing with me later."

The surprised blink and his jaw dropping made regret rise in her throat. *Why did I say that?* Inwardly, she cursed her big mouth and her inability to keep her thoughts from spewing from her lips. She felt her cheeks burning and guessed they were redder than her hair.

She opened her mouth to apologize, but David cut her off with a low guffaw. "I'd be honoured to take you salsa dancing. I may even show you a trick or two," he replied with a grin.

Seeing how his two front teeth overlapped his bottom ones made something—Lauren wasn't sure what—tingle deep in her core, and her heart sighed. A giggle rose in her chest as she put her hand in his and rose to her feet. "Lead the way to the food, before we both starve," she said with a snort.

David lifted her hands to his lips, and a tingle travelled from their entwined fingers to her heart, deep into her core. "As you wish, madam." With a wink, he led her to the buffet, not letting go of her fingers.

CHAPTER FOUR

Ballroom #2
Sunrise Resort, The Bahamas

Salsa dancing came naturally to Joshua. Not many Campbell men of the older generations knew how to dance outside of a few awkward steps while slow dancing or a full waltz, but his uncle Grayson had learned ballroom dancing and more, thanks to Joshua's aunt Abby, who was a dancer in her teens. They taught their son and any of their nieces and nephews who were interested. Joshua had been one of their first students, being only four when he started dancing along with his siblings Angela and Jason, as well as his cousins Levi and Tanya, and of course, Ewan.

He eased Lauren around in a spin, holding her hand above her head, and her green skirt whirled around her legs as she whipped around twice, facing him, and the fingers on her other hand found his. Her eyes twinkled happily up at him as their fronts brushed briefly. A giggle escaped her lips, barely audible over the sound of the upbeat tune blaring from the speakers thirty feet to Joshua's left.

The band ended the tune and started up another one, a faster yet just as peppy beat.

Joshua leaned forward and almost yelled into her ear, "Another round, or do you want to rest?"

Lauren grinned at him, her eyes sparkling in the lights flashing around the dance area. "Let's go sit down. I need a break after that last set."

He let go of one of her hands and started guiding her off of the floor toward the tables to their right. Their table was a ways from the dancing, in a quieter area of the ballroom. He had chosen it to give himself and Lauren some privacy if they wished to chat at any point during the night.

Without letting go of her fingers, he pulled her chair out, and with a small sigh, she dropped into her seat, giving his hand a quick squeeze before she loosened her grip. He immediately dropped his hand, feeling a weird sensation, as though he'd lost something as her fingers left his.

He shrugged it off and flopped down on the chair next to hers. "Having fun?" he asked, prompting a huge smile from her.

"I haven't enjoyed an evening like this in years." She giggled and lifted her glass, which boasted the typical limes and mint leaves of a mojito, and took a sip. "I never expected you to be so light on your feet. Who taught you to dance like that?"

His ears started to warm up as he replied, "My aunt Abby. She was a dance instructor and taught me and a lot of my cousins when we were teenagers."

She blinked and set her glass down. "You weren't out, causing trouble with your friends?"

Heat spread from his ears to his cheeks. "Not always. Sometimes we'd get a snowstorm, and my parents didn't like us going too far. I grew up close to both of my aunts and uncles' houses, so we'd either ski or walk over to one of their places to alleviate the boredom. Sometimes hanging out with one of the cousins was a lot more fun than being bored at home." He lifted his sparkling water—orange flavoured—and took a long drink from it. The scent of citrus wafted around him, almost masking the scents of sweat, tobacco smoke and marijuana smoke from other patrons in the bar area.

"How many cousins do you have?" she asked, her voice barely audible above the din.

Collin's voice at the back of his mind, telling him to be discreet about his true identity, rose in his mind again. With a hope that a vague answer would suffice, he responded, "Enough to please my grandparents." He gestured toward her with his left hand. "Where did you learn to dance?"

Her face flushed, almost as scarlet as her hair. "I took lessons." There was a sheepish note in her voice.

"Lessons? How long ago?" He narrowed his eyes at her with a smirk, guessing it wasn't that long since she learned salsa dancing. She looked too embarrassed to have known it that long.

Her eyes rolled skyward and she giggled awkwardly. "Um, about a week before I got here."

He nodded and snickered. "I wondered, considering how you kept looking at our feet every couple of minutes."

Her azure eyes went wide and she slapped her right hand over her face. "Was I that obvious?" Embarrassment flowed out of every word.

Joshua couldn't hide his mischievous grin. "The sun wasn't as noticeable as you were."

She sighed, folded her arms on the table and rapped her forehead against the metal. "Leave it to me to pick someone experienced enough to see it in a partner."

Mirth rose in his throat, and a loud guffaw slipped from his lips. "I should have warned you after I saw you looking for the third time, but I didn't think you'd want me to call you out on it."

She lifted her head to meet his gaze, and a guilty smile spread across her face. "I never thought to mention it. Most guys don't know how to dance, so I didn't think it was necessary. Next time, I think I'll just sit it out on the sidelines, or not tango with the pros. Just regular, random stuff."

Unable to resist teasing her, he leaned forward and hiked an eyebrow. "Random stuff? Like what?" He added a strong jesting tone to his words so she'd know he wasn't serious.

She giggled and rolled her eyes again. With a wave of her hand, she said, "You know, just moving to the music like we do for something like a rap song." She awkwardly motioned with her hands, almost as if she was doing a dry doggie paddle over the table.

He shook his head slowly, adding a snicker to get her going. "No, I don't know. Tell me more."

Her eyes widened, her shoulders drooped, and she gave him a dirty look. "Yes, you know. Didn't you dance that way in school, or were you too good for it, Mr. Classical Dancer?" She gave him a light push on his bicep, enough to convey she was teasing him, too.

Classical Dancer? She was going to pay for that one. Sweet, beautiful Lauren had no idea who she was teasing. He'd learned all of the best ways to get someone going, thanks to his older brothers and his cousins Ewan and Dana. One more joke, and she was going down, in flames.

"If you mean slow dances, sure. I did that. But random, whatever-you-call-it?" He gave her a sly glance. "What did you call it?"

Her glare—which he was sure was in jest, because he could see the sides of her mouth twitching as if she was trying not to smile—turned a hint hotter. "I didn't call it anything other than dancing at school. I didn't know there was a name for it."

He cocked his head to the left, still holding her gaze. "I thought you called it random stuff."

She closed her eyes, let out a long sigh, and shook her head. "Isn't that what teenage dancing is? Random stuff?"

"Not unless you're a classical dancer like me," he muttered with a snort.

Her lids lifted and her cerulean gaze held his again as she let out a long growl. After a moment, her eyes narrowed and she leaned forward, her hand on her chin. "Stop teasing me, David." She poked him in the chest with her other hand.

He couldn't stop the smirk from forming. "Teasing you? Why do you think I'm teasing you?" It was hard not to laugh at her widening eyes, blank stare, and finally, the middle finger that flew into his vision.

He allowed a single short snicker out of his throat. "I'd never tease someone I barely knew," he added when she blinked at him slowly several times.

She repeated the rude gesture, her hand an inch from his nose. The sudden strong urge to kiss her fingers and tease her in another way rose in his gut, and an image of her face after he kissed her lips burned across his mind. He closed his eyes, making the image scorch the inside of his eyelids for a few more seconds.

A shudder of something travelled through his gut, down his spine, and lodged deep in his groin. Heat settled in every nerve cell, and a tenderness slid through his brain.

He wasn't attracted to her, was he? Lauren was a beautiful woman, sweet, funny, and sensual, but he wasn't ready for anything other than friendship. Not yet. Sybil was dead barely a year and three months. Shouldn't he be still mourning her?

A jolt reminded him that he would mourn her for the rest of his days, but like his father Lukas reminded him, he was still alive, and there was no reason for him not to go on living. Sybil would have understood if he had met someone else and moved on.

"Were you thinking about your wife?" Lauren's soft gentle inquiry penetrated his mind. She touched his forearm, her fingers warm, light and soothing.

He let out a long exaggerated breath and opened his eyes to meet her gaze again. She cocked her head to the side, curiosity oozing out of her movements. He covered her fingers with his and gave hers a soft squeeze and a small smile. "I'm all right."

She smiled sadly at him. "It's okay if you think about her. She was a big part of your life, and you did love her."

He nodded and squeezed her fingers again. "I did, but she wouldn't want me to be sad. Sybil wasn't like that." He glanced down at their now entwined fingers and chuckled. "She was the kind of person who cried for a bit, then moved on with her life. She always said life was too short to be down in the dumps every day."

Lauren's smile got brighter. "She must have been a smart and wise woman."

He grinned and shrugged. "Yeah, she was. She was also one of the most down to earth people I ever met."

"I wish I had known her." There was a lot of gentleness in Lauren's tone.

He lifted his gaze to hers again and went with what his gut said. "She would have liked you, a lot. She loved people who made her laugh, and I think you would have had her in stitches."

Her gaze looked a little watery as she smiled and replied, "I'm honoured. I think I would have loved her, too."

Their gaze held across a foot of white metal table, and the sounds, smells and sights around them faded into the distance the longer they scrutinized each other. He could almost feel something building, something tenuous, that if allowed to grow, would develop into something big, larger than he had ever experienced.

Without thinking, he leaned forward and let himself taste her lips, just the barest of touches. Tingles of pleasure shot through his mouth, deep into his groin, and lastly his heart. The tremble of her lower lip against his sent shockwaves of joy through his soul.

He was attracted to her, in an almost explosive kind of way, and he knew the instant he felt the silkiness of her mouth under his that he was coming back into the light and his heart was starting to live again, for this amazing woman he barely knew.

Lauren's soft gasp and a firm pressure against his mouth told him she was affected, too, but was it as strongly as he had been?

He opened his eyes, pulled back an inch, and stared deep into her eyes again.

A blush spread across her cheeks, and she reached up to touch his lips with her fingers. "Well," she mouthed and cleared her throat. "I never expected that."

Heat spread across his face. "Neither did I." A glance at her mouth had him craving the feel of her again, but he held back.

She giggled softly with a quick smile and rubbed his bottom lip with her thumb.

Her touch sent a tingle of delight through him, joy from her touch, and relief that she hadn't told him to take a hike. He liked her, too much, and it was dizzying how fast it had gone from just knowing her face to their first, and hopefully not their last, kiss.

She leaned forward, but a woman screaming at the start of the next number started them. Lauren pulled back, and although disappointed, Joshua smiled at her.

She brushed her fingers along his jaw and one corner of her mouth lifted. "Do you feel like showing me more of those dance moves?"

He grinned and stood up, holding a hand out to her. "Any time you want."

She slid her hand into his and rose to her feet gracefully with a smile.

CHAPTER FIVE

The next morning
Poolside Buffet

Joshua was at his usual table for brunch, sipping his first cup of coffee that morning, when someone flopped down on the chair to his left, leaned forward to put their head on their folded arms, and let out a long groan.

"Me and my dumb ideas," Lauren muttered, barely audible over the din surrounding them. Her sunhat hid her face, but he could hear a bit of pain in her voice.

His cousin Dana's first time getting drunk blinked in his mind, because Lauren sounded just like Dana had that morning. "Are you okay?" he asked, to be sure she wasn't coming down with something.

She lifted her head. Sunglasses covered her eyes, her face was so pale that her freckles looked painted on, and even her lips looked white. She let out a long, pained breath and groaned. "Coffee. I need coffee."

With a shake of his head and a snicker, Joshua shoved an already filled mug her way, made up just the way she liked. Instead of getting just his own cup filled, he'd got one for her, too, so they could chat while they fulfilled their mutual need for caffeine.

She grasped it like it was her only lifeline and took three long gulps. A small burp escaped her lips, making her jump, but it brought some colour into her face. She lowered her hand, showing the empty mug. She groaned again and put her free hand over her eyes. "Fucking sun. Why can't we have one cloudy day for a change?"

He raised an eyebrow at her. "You had two drinks last night. How did you get hung over?" They had parted ways at midnight the night before, once he started feeling exhaustion kicking in. Or that's what he'd told Lauren.

Thankfully Lauren had been kind and kissed his cheek before they parted ways in the lobby. He'd then ridden up the elevator to his floor after she ran into the people she'd had met a few days ago in the lobby. If she hadn't promised him she was going to hang out with the others, he would have taken her to her own room before retiring to his.

In reality, their unexpected kiss had him yearning for something he wasn't sure if he was ready for. Joshua was a loner when he needed to think something over, and he couldn't think when Lauren was beside him, her sweet and delightful chatter echoing in his ears, and the smell of her ocean-scented perfume wafted up his nose.

He wasn't ready to let go of Sybil, not yet, but somehow, something deep inside of him was screaming for him to start moving on and living his life. It was something so primal, so deeply buried, but fighting its way to the surface.

Joshua let out a long breath, took a long sip of his own java and savoured it, swirling across his tongue before swallowing it. Dark Colombian brew was his favourite, and this one carried a hint of vanilla in its aftertaste.

Her sunglasses slid down a notch, just enough for her to glare at him with bleary blue eyes. "We did shooters after you went upstairs."

His left eyelid twitched. "Shooters? What kind?"

She blinked. "I'm not sure. Something cherry-flavoured. I think. We all took turns ordering rounds for everyone." She flopped her head on the table with a wince and grumbled, "I should have stopped after the second one. The eighty-nine-year-old man by the bar was looking like a supermodel at that point."

Joshua snorted and laughter bubbled up in his chest. That told him she'd had way too much to drink the night before. A wave of guilt flooded through him for not sticking around to watch over her.

He blinked and shrugged it off. He wasn't her protector — they had only spent a few hours together. She was an adult and completely independent, from what he had seen.

"How many rounds did you do?" He took another long sip of coffee, raising an eyebrow at her when their gazes met over the top of his mug.

She sighed. "Four, I think." She lifted her head, cleared her throat and shoved her sunglasses up enough so she could rub her eyes. No makeup, he noted. She looked pale and tired, but the longer she sat with him, the better she looked. Maybe fresh air and a quick cup of coffee was helping her feel more normal. "I feel like something the cat dragged in."

Without thinking, he leaned forward and gently tweaked her nose with his right hand. "You don't look like a dead mouse. More like a sick skunk."

She gave him something akin to a mock glare and swiped his arm. "I feel like a fucking drowned rat, though."

He glanced at the pool, at her, and back to the blue water again. "No, but I could arrange for you to look like one." He added a teasing note to his voice and grinned at her. Joking around with her was easy—she was quick on the comebacks and wasn't afraid to toss him a few rude gestures along the way.

Another mock scowl from her made a snort escape his lips.

"Try it, and your balls will be hanging out of your nose, sunshine," she muttered. She lifted her right hand, her middle finger standing straight up about an inch from his face.

He snorted in laughter again and pushed her hand away.

"Eh, I'm too hungry to waste time on rescuing you, anyway. What do you want for breakfast?"

Her face turned a lovely shade of olive before she flopped her head down on the table again. "Do they serve morphine?" Her voice was muffled by her hat, which had gone askew when she did the face-plant into the glass tabletop.

"Morphine? How bad is it?" Worried, Joshua pulled the hat from her head and tossed it aside so he could look at her. He ran his hand across the side of her head, the velvety silk of her curls sliding between his fingers in a caress. He found her chin with his fingers and lifted her face to his. With his free hand, he removed her sunglasses and stared deep into her cerulean gaze. She was pale, with dark circles and puffiness around her face, but her gaze was clear and her face didn't feel warm. Neither did her forehead when he lightly pressed the inside of his forearm against it. "You don't have a fever," he stated and cocked his head to his right.

"I'm okay. I just have a *headache*," she shot back, one eyebrow rising under his scrutiny before their gazes locked.

She blinked at him a few times, her breathing tickling the pad of his thumb and her gaze softening. The corners of her lips rose a few notches before she pulled back and planted a quick kiss on his fingers.

Something, some unnamed emotion zinged through his groin and landed in his heart, as did something he recognized from the night before.

An image of them entwined in his bed, with her glorious crimson hair spread out around her as he fucked her within an inch of her life hit him so hard, it made a visible shudder travel through his entire system, producing a painful erection.

Fuck, he was attracted to this redheaded pixie, so much so that he wanted to bury himself balls-deep inside of her and never come out of her.

Her eyes went wide for the briefest of seconds, as though

she'd felt the jolt, too. She licked her lips, making them glisten in the glare off of the pool, and attracting his gaze.

Hell, he wanted to come in her mouth, her pussy, all over her, wherever she wanted him to release his desire for her.

She bit her lower lip, then glanced down at his mouth before bringing her gaze to his again. He wasn't sure who moved first, but he could see her face getting a little closer —

Something hit the back of his chair, startling him. He let out a surprised yelp as something cold coated him and splashed on Lauren. "Ah!"

"Uh oh! I'm so sorry, sir." A young girl about seven or eight years old skidded to a stop beside their table, her brown pigtails bouncing as she blinked up at him. "Michaela threw the ball, and I didn't catch it. I didn't mean for it to hit you."

Joshua let out a long breath as he smiled at her. Relieved it had been an accident, even though he was soaked to the skin, he chuckled and picked up his somewhat dry cloth napkin with the yellow *Sunrise Retreat* logo embroidered on it. "It's okay," he said around a chuckle. "Accidents happen." He located the ball in question and rolled it to the youngster. "Go on, go have some fun. Just be a bit more careful about your aim next time."

She beamed at him. "Thanks!" With a bob of her braids, the child scampered off, holding her prized ball and letting out a happy squeal as she leaped into the somewhat crowded pool.

He moved his gaze back to Lauren, who looked like she was trying to hide a grin. "What?"

"You're soaked," she murmured, scooping up her own napkin and dabbing at his face with it. Her lips twitched and her eyes looked brighter than they had a few minutes ago.

"So? It's part of the risk of eating by a pool filled with a bunch of kids," he retorted.

A smile flashed across her face for a moment. "If you want to get changed, I can wait. We can meet up later, maybe at the ballroom this evening."

He frowned. The thought of not spending the entire day with her suddenly made him feel ill, like he'd be missing out on something special. "I have a better idea." He leaned forward so there was barely two inches of space between their faces. "Since I'm already soaked, why don't we go change into our bathing suits and go snorkelling? We can eat after we're done."

A smile spread across her face and she nodded slowly. "Let me take some aspirin, and let's go for a walk first. I want that to kick in before I go swimming, in case the water makes it worse."

Elation rose through his gut as he rose to his feet and held out a hand for her. "Perfect."

CHAPTER SIX

The view under the crystal-clear water off of the resort's private beach was spectacular. Lauren had never seen such an assortment of unusual and beautiful wildlife in a single spot since her last foray to the provincial wildlife park in Shubenacadie, only a few weeks ago, and most of the wildlife there were land-dwelling animals like bobcats and wolves, or shore-dwelling animals like otters and beavers.

The atoll was several hundred feet offshore, behind an outcropping of rocks, and hosted life from coral growing on the former liner to lionfish, plenty of stingrays, and a lot more species she didn't recognize. The water was so warm and silky along her skin that wasn't covered by her one-piece suit, and it felt wonderful to paddle along, mesmerized by the enchanting view below her.

However, all that beauty didn't compare to the man whose hand she was holding as they navigated the reef, not too far from the rocks in that small area of the Atlantic Ocean.

He squeezed her fingers, a signal they had worked out as a means of alerting each other to something. She glanced at David, who pointed toward something ahead of them. He smiled around his mouthpiece, and she could see his wink behind his goggles.

She turned her head and almost gasped when she saw the dolphin with a calf swimming ahead of them, the baby riding along behind its mother's dorsal fin. It was heartwarming. They were careful to keep their distance. Dolphins were common around her home province, but she had never seen any of them with a baby in tow before.

She looked back at him, grinning around her mouthpiece, and noticed he was watching the mother and baby navigating away from them. He turned, his eyes almost black in the shadows of the water, their gazes meeting through their goggles, sending a jolt of awareness deep into her soul, her core—and her heart.

Vertigo slammed into her chest as the realization she wanted to have sex with him rose in her throat. She wanted to explore every single inch of his tan skin, from the top of his head to his toes, and every millimetre in between. She wanted to feel his balls slapping her ass as he fucked her within an inch of her life, taste his cum on her tongue, and smother him with her pussy as she rode his face.

Her core immediately tightened, and she could feel the evidence of her desire seeping out between her lower lips. Her nipples went from flat to poking upwards, in a demand for him to remove the top of her suit and lick her breasts into oblivion.

She stopped paddling and began treading water. He, too, halted, and fully turned to face her.

Their bodies brushed together under the warm water, sending a deeper awareness of him through her body and her soul. He put his hands on her waist, pulling her closer to him so they were touching from chest to knees. His gaze burned through his diving mask into hers as their faces nuzzled together under the water, their snorkels not inhibiting their play, but enhancing their need to touch and be touched.

Something rigid touched Lauren's lower abdomen. She shifted upwards, and felt the tip of it brush the top edge of her slit, sending a zap of lust through her pussy and into her heart. Lauren put her hands on his shoulders, wrapped her legs around his waist, and thrust her hips against his, feeling more than hearing his groan of pleasure.

Fuck, he wanted her as much as she wanted him. Was that why he'd kissed her last night, and wanted her to come snorkelling with him?

Lauren realized she hadn't cared about his motives for asking her to join him that day. All that mattered was being together in that second in time, and whatever happened after that moment would change their lives forever.

He kicked at the water, and seconds later, they broke the surface. Water sluiced down his face and he flipped his braid over his shoulder. He pulled his goggles off of his face and spit out the mouthpiece of the snorkel. Her goggles were shoved upwards, and her own mouthpiece removed. A heartbeat later, he was crushing his mouth against hers.

Lauren parted her lips for him, his tongue thrusting into her mouth as they floated locked together. She squeezed her legs around his waist, feeling his dick scraping along the crotch of her bathing suit. His low groan echoed in her ears, and a second later, she felt his fingers move from her waist to her slit, caressing it through the wet material. Something hard pushed against her back, indicating he had moved them toward a safer haven, preferably out of view of the beach and anyone swimming.

With a hope no one saw them, she pressed her pussy into his hand, moaned and thrust her tongue deeper into his mouth, a signal to continue.

He must have understood, because a moment later, the crotch of her swimsuit was eased aside and something hot and rigid pressed against the outer lips of her core.

Desire burned through her veins, fogging her mind and taking over every cell of her body. The thought of *no condoms* flickered through her mind for a nanosecond before her instincts took over and she ground her pussy against the head of his cock, feeling its head easily slide into her entrance.

He pulled back and stared deep into her eyes, his gaze

black with lust and desire, a question in his look.

She squeezed her internal muscles and whispered in a husky voice, "Fuck me, David. Fuck me until I can't think."

His entire body shuddered for a moment—then he let out a long, deep hiss and pushed his hips forward.

God, he was big. Lauren felt her pussy stretching a bit to accommodate his width, but oh, did it ever feel amazing to have him inside of her. She tightened around him, felt his cock twitching, and as he held himself still inside of her, she felt her climax building.

Another thrust as he held her steady brought her closer to her peak.

"David, I'm going to—god, I can't stop it," she whimpered against his lips, her orgasm a heartbeat away.

He nodded and ground his teeth together, giving her another hard, quick thrust and stiffening for a moment as she rode the wave of her delight, squeezing his dick and almost screaming her pleasure into his mouth.

She had barely finished when the fullness of his cock slid out of her and its length pressed against her clit, sending an aftershock of pleasure through her as his own spasms began, exploding his seed into the water between their bodies.

Shaking, they pulled back to stare into each other's eyes again, and Lauren could feel the connection they had solidifying into an unbreakable bond. Whatever had drawn them together and prompted this unexpected round of lustful play—in a public venue of all places—sank into her heart and her soul.

At that moment, she realized that she could never forget him. Whatever happened after she went home, this wonderful, kind and sexy man would always be in her heart.

Joshua trembled as he lowered his face to Lauren's, the aftershocks of their combined lust continuing between them, her pussy shuddering in time with his pulsing member. The warmth of the water, the heat of the sun, and the feel of rocks against his knees and under his feet started penetrating his brain, but what had just happened sent shockwaves of surprise and fear into his core.

Holy fuck. They had just had unprotected sex, in a public spot of all places. What the hell possessed him to make love to Lauren, and without a condom? He hadn't been with anyone since he started dating Sybil fourteen years ago, so Lauren was safe from any STDs.

But what about pregnancy? If she wasn't on the pill or anything else, he could have easily knocked her up. *Shit. How stupid could I get?*

This wasn't supposed to happen.

He stared deep into her eyes and realized that their coupling had been inevitable. He had been drawn to her from the moment he laid eyes on her magnificent body her first day at the resort and couldn't stay away from her if he had tried.

The lava of regret burned every single one of his nerve endings. "Lauren, sweetheart, I—"

She reached up to touch his lips with her fingers and shook her head, her snorkel banging the side of her head and the rocks behind her. "If you apologize for moving so fast, I'll hit you. I wanted this as much as you did," she whispered.

It cooled his remorse, but only a little. "I should have taken my time, and waited another day or two before we went this far," he replied softly.

Her lips caressed his, sending a huge wave of an unnamed emotion through his body, into his heart and his soul. "It wouldn't have mattered if we'd waited or not. It was going to happen sooner or later." She slid her arms around his neck, and her legs tightened around his waist, pulling his hips against hers.

Jesus, just the feel of her body was making him hard again, and so soon after their initial lust had been satisfied. "I should have used birth control, just to be safe. What if you—"

Lauren nuzzled her face against his. "I'm on the pill, so there's a good chance that won't happen."

Relief zinged through him. He relaxed and placed a soft kiss on her lips. "Still, I'd rather use condoms from now on, to be doubly safe. I'd rather not have something happen, if you know what I mean."

She smiled and hugged him tight. "I understand, and it's okay. I'm not ready for motherhood yet. Besides it's still pretty soon after your wife died. How long has it been since you've been with anyone?"

Heat spread across his cheeks, down his neck, and into his ears. "I haven't been with anyone else since I started dating her, and she died a year ago last August," he mumbled, turning his head to stare at the water rippling against the rocks.

She touched his chest, over his heart. "I'm sorry," she murmured, tightening her arms around his neck and hugging him tightly.

It felt odd talking about Sybil with another woman, especially after he'd just had sex with her, but it also felt right telling Lauren about his late wife and how much he missed her.

Maybe he had lost his mind thanks to the booze after all?

The thought flew away when he turned his face to meet her gaze, where he saw compassion and some unnamed emotion floating in her eyes. He nodded marginally and cleared his throat a few times before shifting so he could rest his head on her shoulder.

She hugged him tighter and sighed. "It's over six months for me. My ex was fucking my best friend and decided he liked her better than me."

There was a lot of snark and hate in her tone, so much he lifted his head to stare at her intently. Her eyes were cold, and her perfect lips were curled into a sneer.

He kissed her softly in hopes of erasing the hate he saw spitting out of her expression and her animated azure gaze. Her mouth opened under his and her tongue extended into his mouth as he slowly tried kissing her anger away.

He didn't lift his head until he felt her relaxing and almost melting in his arms. Her eyes were back to their regular warmth, and she was smiling.

"You're so good to me," she whispered.

Something rose in his chest at her words—pride, lust, affection, and so many nameless feelings that hit him between the eyes.

Shit. He liked her—a lot. Maybe way too much after some fun in the tropical sunlight.

A shudder travelled through him as it all became clear.

He didn't want this to be a fling, he wanted more.

He didn't want to go home alone after this trip.

He wanted to tell her everything—about his alcoholism, his family, his real name, and anything else she wanted to know about him.

He wanted to take her home to Alberta with him and see if whatever was going on between them was a temporary lust-filled attraction, or something more permanent.

To hell with what his family said, he was going to tell her the truth. Lauren deserved to know it, and more.

She moved her lower body against his, and his dick went from half flaccid to rock hard.

He'll tell her—once they relieved their lust a few more times.

His vow to come clean with her went silent when she pushed him back a little and started caressing his balls before sliding away under the water. He slid his member into a hot cavity, and a suction combined with something caressing the head of his dick made a low, gasping groan escape his mouth.

All thoughts were forgotten as lust permeated his entire being.

CHAPTER SEVEN

Lauren had changed into a sundress, no bra or panties, grabbed her purse, and tossed some things into a small bag, just enough to spend the night with him.

A tremor travelled through her as she added a few toiletries and a comb. She doubted makeup or anything else would be necessary once the door of his room closed behind her, maybe not even clothing.

However, she didn't want to leave him too long, now that they were having sex, so just a few necessary things were required. There was no question she wasn't leaving his room until morning.

If not later than that.

A zap of pleasure and lust zinged through her core and into her heart when she recalled the look in his eyes as he'd entered her. It was pure ecstasy, although something else flickered in his gaze from time to time. Something she couldn't pinpoint.

Her hands stilled, despite her haste to get to his room. Something surged in her from deep within her soul, making her sigh and her knees turn to jelly.

She didn't just lust after David. She *liked* him. He was kind, considerate, gentle, polite and classy to the bone—unlike Dorian.

She had more orgasms in one session with David than she had in three years with her slimy ex-husband. He'd rarely touched her in the last year of their marriage, she had noticed, only when he couldn't see his side piece.

An image of David smiling at her before kissing her hand rose in her mind. Everything he did for her, from getting her a coffee, to holding her chair out, and asking permission to make love to her made her anger at Dorian and Mallory evaporate.

If she hadn't caught them a few months ago, she wouldn't have been at this resort, enjoying this special time and the most amazing man she had ever known. For that, she had to thank them. A giggle escaped her lips as she pictured the looks on their faces when they opened a thank you card from her, for allowing her to move on with her life and find someone special to call her own.

Another jolt sent a shockwave of warmth into her soul.

She didn't want to go home alone. The thought of returning home without him made her feel sick.

She wanted to take David with her, to show him her beloved province of Nova Scotia, her childhood haunts and more. She wanted to walk on the ocean floor with him, show him the tides of her favourite beach, and dance with him under the lights during the Apple Blossom Festival in the spring.

Lauren felt tears spring into her eyes, and she wiped them away.

If she wasn't careful, she'd fall for David—and fast.

She only hoped he wouldn't break her heart, because it would never recover.

Less than thirty seconds after she knocked, he opened his room door. His beautiful eyes crinkled at the corners as he smiled, showcasing his straight, white teeth, and how the left side of his mouth rose higher than the right.

Her heart sighed when their gazes met. Bashfulness rose in her chest, but she shoved it down and stepped over the threshold of his private area.

A quick glance around showed he had a suite, but the layout was the opposite of hers. They were in a living area, with the same blue, white and yellow themed prints, soft blue carpet, pale yellow furniture, and white walls with blue trim around the windows and the patio doors, which lead to a small balcony. A large smart TV hung on the wall opposite the couch and loveseat, with dark varnished accoutrements, like a coffee table, two other side tables and a cabinet for the mini bar, which she noted was closed.

He moved to stand by her, and she turned to stare up at him.

He was not much taller than she was in her three-inch heels, maybe an inch or so. She could see out of the corner of her eye that his chest was bare, his skin a little darker than it had been a few days ago, although his ribs didn't seem as prominent as they had been the first day they met, which was good. She didn't mind a man being slim, but he had been too skinny for her comfort.

The thought of her and her mother making sure he was well fed and more if she took him home with her flashed through her mind.

She could feel her cheeks heat up while they scrutinized each other. Lust, tenderness and more swelled in her chest, the emotions rampaging through her entire body and zapping her hard in her core.

He took a step forward, the front of his body brushing hers. A gasp escaped her throat, pleasure zinging through her breasts, through her abdomen and deep inside of her pussy. Sweat slid along the back of her knees, in her hair, and she could feel wetness sliding out between her lower lips. Her nipples puckered, poking him in the chest through the thin material of her dress.

Shit. She was horny, and going by how she could feel something pressing against her stomach, he was, too.

She opened her mouth to ask him if he had condoms—

But was stopped when he crushed his mouth against hers and tugged at her dress.

Fuck! The man could kiss. Just the feel of his mouth over hers was making her slit go crazy, producing moisture, and the feel of his hands on her bare hips under her dress had her entire body screaming for him to fill her.

He pulled back for a moment. "Get this off," he commanded softly with a low groan, shoving the material up her ribcage.

She lifted her arms, and the blue cotton covered her face for a moment before disappearing. David tossed it over his shoulder and his gaze lowered to her chest.

He took a single step backwards, letting his gaze roam her body from her neck to her breasts, from her waist to her feet, then finally linger on the trimmed red hair shadowing her pussy.

Her nipples got tighter, her knees turned to jelly, and she could feel her body heating up under his appraisal. She glanced at his waist—all he had on was a white towel with the hotel's logo embroidered on it, and it was tented in the front.

He moved his gaze to hers. Smouldering lust reflected out of his deep brown eyes, the intensity of his desire for her zapping her soul with ten million volts.

"You're so fucking beautiful." He groaned, lifting his hands to capture her breasts in his palms.

A long painful *zap* penetrated Lauren's core and spread out to encompass every nerve ending, heightening her hunger for him and her desire to please him.

One of his hands left her body for a moment, and his towel dropped to the floor. With a slow blink at him, she moved her gaze downward to his dick.

He wasn't as long as Dorian, but he was thicker. Black hair

surrounded his erect cock, and with a thrill of wonder, Lauren noted he wasn't circumcised. She'd thought he wasn't, going by how he had felt in her mouth as she gave him a fellatio, but hadn't been sure. Things were too clouded by lust to remember much from their play on the rocks, other than how they had fucked and she had played with his dick for a bit before returning to the hotel and planning her overnight stay with him in his suite.

Fuck! She needed him inside of her—again and again—until they were so spent, they couldn't move.

She shifted her gaze up his slim waist to his chest and saw he was tan where his swim trunks had covered, a bit lighter than the parts that had been exposed to the sun. Another glance downward showed slim legs, with slight bulges of muscle, and no hair on most of his body, other than a bit on his forearms, under his arms, and around his balls, which looked heavy and tight with desire.

She raised her eyes again, moving so their bare bodies touched from chest to knees for the first time. A heartbeat later, he grabbed her ass, lifted her off of her feet, and claimed her mouth with his. He rubbed his dick against her pussy hair, a tease that sent millions of volts of pleasure into her being.

She felt herself being lowered onto her back, the soft velvety material of the couch caressing her rear, and her legs dangled over the edge. She spread them as far as she could, allowing him full access to her throbbing core and plenty of room for him to look at her.

She slid her eyes shut and lifted her hips, demanding him, now. "David, please. Fuck me," she demanded, her voice sounding loud in the quiet room.

"Soon," he hissed, and a moment later, moisture rubbed against her pussy, parting her lips and sliding around her entrance.

Pleasure roared in her slit, making her wetter, and a cry escaped her lips. A nanosecond later, suction on her clit had her arching her back and wrapping her legs around his head. "Oh god!" she cried, pushing her pussy deeper into his face, demanding more of his ministrations.

More suction and a finger sliding along her asshole made her scream in delight. "Damn it, don't do that, I'm on the verge of coming," she whimpered, unable to catch her breath. It was so hard not to screech, or to smother him by ramming herself into his face so hard he wouldn't be able to breathe.

A few hard slow licks left her whimpering in frustration. "Let me come, dammit," she moaned, wriggling on the couch, and almost falling off.

One longer, unhurried move against her clit made a long, loud cry pass from her mouth. She felt him pulling back, opened her eyes, and looked down at him.

He rose to his knees and their gazes met. His head was between her shaking thighs, his lips parted, and he placed a soft kiss on her slit. The pure lust in his gaze made her heart skip a few beats and race with the knowledge that she affected him so strongly.

He moved her legs from his body and grabbed something on the couch beside her. "Stay put," he commanded and a second later, she heard the sound of a package being ripped open.

A fleeting thought that he had purchased condoms went through her mind a split second before he grabbed her hips, pulled her toward him, and rubbed her clitoris with his fingers.

Pleasure tore through her entire being again, this time her legs went around his waist and she yanked him toward her. "Now," she pled with him, sinking her fingers into his ass and arcing her back.

With a long, hard, thrust, David entered her, filling her

completely, his balls slapping her ass. She locked her legs around his waist. This time there would be no pulling out, no worrying if she would get pregnant or anything else. She was going to feel his dick letting loose inside of her via the safety of the condom, hopefully more than once that day.

She moaned, grinding her hips against his, squeezing his cock with her Kegel muscles and thrusting her breasts into the air. She shut her eyes, and a moment later, a wet heat hit her nipple, while he grazed the other one with a calloused palm, sending her pleasure into the stratosphere.

David pulled back a little before plunging into her again, the head of his dick scraping the inside of her sheath at the point where her pleasure would be the highest. His hand left her breast, and something slid between them, along her slit, to touch the one spot she'd gain the maximum pleasure. A long, hard shot of pure delight ripped through her body. "Please, David. Make me come," she ground out, her head rolling from side to side on the couch.

He let out a long growl and a moment later, he pushed himself deeper inside of her, his balls hitting her ass again. Another thrust and she was ready to scream. His movements picked up, faster and faster. Unable to hold back anymore, she pushed herself into him, tightening her pussy walls around his dick and wrapping her legs around his waist as she allowed herself to ride the wave of a breath-stealing, world-shattering peak. Her scream of pleasure ripped out of her throat a bare second before she felt him go rigid, his cock exploding inside of her hot channel, his low shout muffled against her neck as he, too, came.

Joshua rose to his elbows and stared down into Lauren's eyes. Her gaze was dreamy, her normally pale cheeks were flushed, hiding her freckles, and her lips were parted as she gulped air. He could feel her inner walls twitching around his still shuddering cock, and smell their combined sweat mixed with the scent of her juices lingering around him. He licked his lips, tasting her on his skin. A smugness rose in his chest when she smiled at him and caressed his cheek with her right hand, which he took into his own hand, placing a soft kiss on the palm.

Still shaking from the most intense and satisfying orgasm he'd had since his last night with Sybil, Joshua leaned forward to kiss Lauren, his fingers tangling in her hair. "You okay?" he murmured against her mouth. His dick was soft and already sliding out of her. He wasn't ready to leave her, not yet. He had to have this moment with her, in the afterglow of their lovemaking, with him still feeling her pussy shuddering from time to time.

She rubbed her hand up and down his upper left arm, caressing his tattoo there. "Yeah. I'm perfect." She eyed the ink under his skin and flicked her thumb against it. "What kind of tattoo is that? I've never seen one in that design before."

He glanced at it with a smile. "It's a bear paw, done in the style of my nation."

Her smile got bigger. "You're Indigenous? What nation?"

He hesitated, his grandfather and father's words about keeping things to himself echoing in his ears.

Lauren frowned and started to pull back, her eyes darkening with sadness. "It's okay. If you don't want me to know . . . " She moved to sit up and let go of him with her legs. He slid out of her, his body feeling so cold and loneliness penetrating his entire being when her warmth left him.

Anger at his family's warnings to keep to himself, especially after having amazing sex with this warm, loving and amazing lady, rose in Joshua's chest.

To hell with protecting the family name. They can go take a flying fuck over the Pacific Ocean. The only thing he wanted was for Lauren to be happy and comfortable with him. If the family didn't like it, they could go fuck themselves.

He put a hand on her leg to stop her, and whispered, "I'm Siksika."

She stopped and stared up at him. "Blackfoot?"

He met her gaze and nodded. "Yeah." He shifted and took her hand in his. "That doesn't bother you, does it?"

She sank down to the couch again, her gaze softening and her lips curving into a smile. "No, it doesn't. A person's race doesn't matter to me, as long as they're a good person. It does explain your beautiful cheekbones and the colour of your skin, along with that tattoo." She touched his chest with a finger, drawing a line toward his belly button. "Do you attend pow-wows or anything else for your tribe?"

Heat spread across his cheeks as embarrassment for his family's lack of Indigenous traditions reverberated in his mind. "No. We are Indigenous in name and our language. But we were raised like we were white, because we have no status, and it's what my family wanted." A thought of his two eastern cousins popped into his mind. "There are a few that are learning our ways, but most of the family rejects our traditions and more." He frowned, remembering his grandfather's rage when he found out about his cousin Ewan and his family learning the Siksika ways, and how Ewan's son Isaiah was hoping to become a pow-wow dancer at some point, even though the child was only three years old.

He let go of the memory and gave Lauren one of his best smiles. "We'll talk about that later. Are you thirsty? I can order a mojito or something else from room service. My treat."

Lauren gave him a filthy look a split second before her face turned green. "Not after last night, thanks. I think I'll stick to something non-alcoholic." She leaned forward, placing a small kiss on his mouth and wrapping her arms around his neck again.

He revelled in her closeness and the feel of her bare skin

against his. "Carbonated water, or something else?"

She rolled her eyes skyward for a moment and brushed her breasts against his front. "I'm not thirsty. I'm hungry," she replied huskily, as a sly grin spread across her face. She moved so the apex of her thighs rubbed against his stomach.

Excitement made his cock twitch. "Hungry for what?" he asked, although he could guess her answer, going by how she was rubbing her pussy against him.

She pulled back and stared deep into his eyes. "You. I'm starving for you again, but let's go play in the bedroom, so we have more room." She leaned back, thrusting her breasts toward his face, an enticing manoeuvre he couldn't resist.

With a low, deep groan, he pressed his face into her chest, found a nipple with his lips, and sucked.

CHAPTER EIGHT

Sunlight covered the bed the following morning, hitting Lauren in the face and making her squint. Why was the sun blazing into her brain? Hadn't she closed the blinds last night?

A movement and the sensation of something lying across her waist brought the memories of the previous day to the forefront of her mind.

She wasn't in her room. She realized she was in David's, and he was still asleep beside her.

She shifted, rolling over to her back, and turned her head to look at him as he slumbered.

His eyes were shut, the long, full eyelashes creating crescents on his tan skin, and his mouth was relaxed in sleep. She could feel his nakedness along hers. Their legs were tangled together, and his chest brushed hers with every breath. She could feel his flaccid penis against her leg, feel the weight of his long hair brushing her arm as she snuggled deeper into his embrace.

He tightened his arm around her for a moment and let out a long, soft sigh before nuzzling his face into her hair. "Lauren," he whispered, calling her name.

She kissed his chin. "Mm. What?" She loved the sound of her name on his lips. Even though he was probably still mostly asleep, he remembered who she was and that she was there.

It was a thrill that dinged every nerve ending in her body and hit her soul, hard.

He tightened his arm around her again, this time not letting go for a minute. Under the covers, something started getting larger and harder against her leg.

She nuzzled her face against his and slid a hand down his side to caress his hip.

His eyes opened a slit, the desire in them burning into hers. "Ride me," he ground out, thrusting his dick against her mound, its tip already leaking his lust.

She pushed him onto his back, throwing the covers to their feet, and reaching across him for the box of condoms. "No foreplay?" she asked, pressing a hard kiss on his mouth.

He shook his head, and took the small package out of her hands, ripping it open before hastily donning it. "Too ex-cited."

The pure lust raging in his words and glowing in his gaze sent her own desire into the stratosphere—they were about to have primal, hot, no-nonsense sex.

She swung her leg over his waist, straddling him, letting his cock rest at the edge of her opening. "Tell me you want me to fuck you again," she ordered, her voice cracking with need.

His gaze burned into her as he grabbed her waist, and lifted his hips, impaling her on his cock. "Fuck me again. Fuck me to death, beautiful Lauren. Fuck me until neither of us can think," he said, growling out the words, and started ramming himself deeper into her.

Her mind already clouded with hunger for him, she tangled her legs around his waist, not letting him budge more than an inch away from her, the primal need to satisfy their craving for each other outweighing everything else.

Moments later, she felt him grow inside of her a few seconds before his orgasm exploded and he called her name, causing her to fall over the edge, her pleasure at a peak for longer than she had in the past.

Sated, she fell forward to rest on his chest, his arms tight around her and his gasps for air in the aftermath puffing in her hair.

Lauren relaxed in his arms, snuggling closer to him and drifting toward sleep as one thought popped into her mind.

She was falling for him, fast, and wanted to be with him, no matter whether it was a long-distance thing or not.

With a sigh, she let herself float, and slumber overtook her again.

Joshua was still reeling from the aftermath of their last coupling when he called room service later that morning. He felt sated and happy, yet still wanted to fuck Lauren within an inch of her life.

Like he hadn't done that several times already? Hell, the woman was as needy and generous as he had been. One moment, she was giving him a blow job, and the next, on all fours, demanding he pound her pussy from behind.

He glanced over at her, sitting at the table by the patio doors, sipping a coffee. As much as he wanted to bury himself into her again, he wanted her to eat first, so she'd have energy for any future rounds. Like him, she was wearing a white robe, tied at the waist, and nothing else, not even slippers. Her bare feet peeked out at him from under the table, the blue polish winking at him from time to time in the sunlight. Her hair was loose, puffed up around her face, the crimson spirals highlighted with blond, auburn in the lowlights.

She smiled at him and placed her mug on the table beside her half-empty plate. "What is it?"

God, she was so beautiful. He hadn't beheld a woman like her since Sybil, who had been gorgeous in her own way, and her soul had been as lovely as the rest of her.

Like Sybil, Lauren had one of those soft, gentle souls, but she was more outspoken than and not as compliant as Sybil had been. She was her own person, another true gem in his world.

Losing his wife almost did him in, but he knew if things ended with Lauren before they were ready to say goodbye, it would ring his death knell.

He moved from his chair to crouch on the floor beside her. On a whim, he whispered, "Come home with me."

Her surprised blink and widening eyes made him chuckle. "I'm serious, Lauren. I don't want to go home alone. I can't bear the thought of not seeing you again after we leave here." He reached up to tuck a curl behind her ear, and leaned forward to kiss her softly. "I want to see if there's more to this," he said, gesturing to her and back to him with his right hand and found her fingers with his left, "than just a fling."

Her eyes became watery. "Go home with you?" She giggled around a sniffle. "I was going to ask you the same thing—to come home with *me*."

Elation rose in his chest and smugness made him grin. "You were?"

She nodded, one tear dripping out of her left eye to run down her cheek and drip off of her chin. "I want you to meet my parents, see all of my favourite places, and so much more," she whispered, tears making her voice thick.

Joy leaped in his chest. "I want you to meet my family and everything else, too," he ground out around the lump forming in his throat. He slipped a hand around her neck, pulling her head down to his so he could give her a long, hard kiss.

"This isn't a fling for me," she murmured. "It was about hanging out with a sweet man who was kind to me, but things changed." She touched his mouth with her fingers, and sighed. "Once you kissed me, I was a goner. I didn't want to leave your side."

He kissed her fingers, slowly, one by one. "I wanted this before I kissed you," he admitted softly. "I don't want to leave the resort without you on my arm, you hear?"

He rose to his feet, pulling her up with him. He slid his arms around her and nuzzled his face against hers. "How soon can you get your stuff up here? I don't want to leave your side for more than a few minutes," he said around a grin, jubilation zinging through his entire body and soul as he stared down at her.

Her arms went around his neck and she giggled, her beautiful face lighting up brighter than the sun. "It shouldn't take me too long. I didn't really unpack much."

He kissed her hard, then lifted her off of her feet in a bear hug. Putting her down gently, he patted her ass and murmured, "Go. Get your stuff. I'll call my brother and tell him I'm bringing someone home with me."

She laughed and planted a long, searing kiss on his lips, joy radiating out of her movements and gaze. "I won't be long. Don't you dare disappear."

He brushed his mouth against hers again. "I won't. I promise."

She threw her arms around his neck again, and he hugged her tightly, bliss that she was going to be in his life a lot longer than a few days making him feel dizzy and stoned. "Go, and be fast."

She ran off, and moments later, came back wearing her soft blue sundress, the high heeled sandals sinking into the carpet, her carryall bumping on her hip. She gave him a quick smooch, whispering, "I'll be back in a few. See ya."

He grinned, leaning into the kiss and savouring the feel of her. "Hurry up. I don't want to waste another second without you."

Lauren touched his face with her fingers before she blew him a kiss and slid out the door.

With a long sigh, Joshua realized he hadn't told her his real name yet. Oh well, he could tell her on the plane as they headed toward home.

Chapter Nine

Excitement, joy and the endless possibilities the future held had Lauren in a state of euphoria. She was almost running toward the elevator in her haste to get to her room, pack the few things she had unpacked, and drag them all up to David's suite, three floors above her own.

Anticipation had her grumbling to herself when the elevator took what seemed like forever to get to the floor. She briefly considered taking the stairs until she looked down at her feet and decided against it, not with her mood going so fast. Running down the stairs in heels wasn't a great idea. She'd probably hurt herself, big time.

She crossed her arms and drummed her fingers against her upper arm as she waited.

Finally the stereotypical *ding* one expected, indicating arrival of the elevator, echoed in the hall, and anticipation ran through her body as the doors slowly opened.

Two men, both with dark hair and wearing suits, got off and looked around. They nodded and each gave her a cool, polite smile.

"Hi," she breathily replied, returning the nod as she sauntered into the elevator and turned to face the hall. The men glanced at her for an instant before the doors slid shut and enclosed her in the small area. She hit the number for her floor and let out a long, happy giggle.

David wanted to see where their connection took them, just like she did. She couldn't believe how fast they had become attached to each other, let alone how well-suited they were in bed. He was a generous, kind, sweet, and gentle lover, always making sure she had her pleasure before he had his, and he was always fussing over her, making sure she was comfortable, happy and relaxed.

He was the man she had dreamed of for so long. She'd thought she could bring it out in Dorian, but she had languished in an unhappy marriage for the last year before catching that loser in bed with her former best friend.

David was everything Dorian wasn't, and it made her heart feel light, like she had come home after being away for eons.

She was falling for him—hard—and couldn't believe he felt the same way.

Five minutes later, she was in her room, grabbing everything she had unpacked, tossing it all into her suitcases and her carryall, not bothering to fold it. She'd fold it while helping David pack his things for their trip to his home.

She had no doubt they were going to his place first, *then* hers. He was so eager to have her meet his family that she had to say yes to his place first.

But she had to alert her family so they wouldn't worry. A quick glance at her watch showed it was almost noon there, and her dad would be in his office before heading home for lunch with her mother.

She picked up her cell phone and dialled the number. Three rings, and her mother's voice sounded in her ear. "Lauren, is that you? I wasn't expecting you to call until tomorrow! Is something wrong?" There was a lot of concern in her mother's voice. Being the only daughter and youngest of the family, she'd been fussed over a lot in her younger years and was still the target of the protective side of her family.

Lauren rolled her eyes, even though she was several thousand miles south of her parents. Her mom couldn't see her doing it. "Hi, Mom. Don't worry, nothing is wrong."

Her mother sputtered for a minute before replying. "Then why are you calling? I thought you'd be enjoying laying in the sun, doing nothing. You should be relaxing in the pool or on the beach, not in your room talking to me." There was a scolding note in her mom's voice, which made Lauren's eyes roll again.

With a long, happy sigh, she said happily, "Mom, I may be late coming home from vacation."

"Why? Did something happen? I didn't see any hurricanes or storms heading that way on the weather."

Lauren snorted. Of course her mother was checking the temperatures and other things for the freaking Bahamas, just to be sure her only daughter was safe and sound. "No, there are no storms coming for a few more days, not till after I leave, which will be a day earlier than planned."

"Why are you leaving early? Your father and I told you to stay down there a full ten days—"

"Mom, I met someone!" Lauren almost screamed it over the line, between frustration with her mother's stream of questions and her elation over going home with David.

A nagging voice at the back of her mind whispered she had no clue where he lived, his last name, or much else about him other than his first name, his dead wife's name, and how he was Siksika.

She brushed it off with a reminder to herself to ask him all of those important things after she returned to his room and they started getting ready to pack for traveling to his house.

Wherever that was.

Her mom's questions came to a halt with a surprised yelp. "What?"

"His name is David, and he's so sweet. I'm leaving early to go home with him." Suddenly feeling silly for falling for this wonderful, gentle man so fast, she picked at the bedspread, rubbing its material between her thumb and a finger, feeling the rasp of the white embroidery.

A stunned silence echoed over the line for a long moment. "Well," her mother began, shock reverberating in her voice. "I was not expecting that, especially after that idiotic jerk cheated on you, with your friend of all people."

Her mother's words made her irresponsible decision to have sex with David and go home with him feel even more so, until a vision of him staring deep into her eyes as they pleasured each other came to the forefront of her mind.

No, her impulsiveness wasn't wrong. What had started on the beach a few days ago was growing, deepening and feeling more and more *right* by the second.

She let out a long sigh. "Maybe it was the right time, you know? I can't be alone forever. The divorce was finalized three weeks ago, and it's been over six months since I gave him the boot, and her, too." Tears formed in her eyes and her voice broke. "I never loved him, Mom. He convinced me I did, but looking back, I know I never did."

She took a deep breath, wondering how she could put this without letting her mom know that her lust for David had clouded her judgement enough that she had sex with him without a condom. Her mother would have fainted if she found that out. Being on the pill was fine if you were monogamous, but it didn't protect from STDs. Her mom could have easily jumped to conclusions about David and given Lauren a huge bawling out.

Thirty years old, and her mom still acted like she was a kid some days.

With a reminder that her father was a lot worse for being overly protective, Lauren let out another long sigh and decided to be honest about how she felt about this sweet, gentle man she had only met a few days prior. "There is something between me and David, and it seems to get stronger every time I see him." She cleared her throat, her feelings for him rising in her chest.

"I want to see where this takes me, Mom. I want to know if this is only a short time thing, or something real, more permanent. Please don't get mad at me for wanting to explore something that feels so right." She sniffled, and felt a tear leak out of her eye. She wiped it away. "I have to do this. I feel like I'll be missing out on something beautiful if I don't follow my heart, and it's telling me to run with him, and go wherever this takes us."

Her mother was quiet for a long moment before she let out a long sigh of her own. "I understand. It was the same way with me and your dad, all of those years ago. You go with him, for however long you need to. I'll cover for you at work. Okay?" her mother whispered, her voice soft, comforting and full of understanding.

Lauren felt tears leaking out of her eyes as she murmured, "Thank you, Mom. I love you. Please tell Daddy what's going on and tell him not to worry."

"Oh, you know he will worry. You're his little girl, and he'll be pacing until you call us from wherever your David lives."

A picture of her dad waiting for her by the front door of her childhood home, like he always had when she was in her teens rose in her mind, making her chuckle. "Tell him not to walk too much, he may wear out the floor."

Her mom laughed. "I will. You let us know how things are going. If it no longer feels right, get your butt on a plane heading for home. You hear?"

Lauren grinned through her tears. "I hear. Tell Daddy I love him, too, and tell Lee to suck a cat's balls."

Her mother snorted in her ear. "I will tell your dad. As for your brother, you can tell him yourself when you bring your David home for a visit."

Elation and anxiety about David meeting her parents and her older brother made her heart twitch, either in joy or nervousness. Lauren wasn't sure. She grinned and sighed. "I will. Thanks, Mom. Give my Marmalade kisses for me."

"I already did. He's snoozing by the open window."

A picture of her orange tabby kitten came to her mind. As much as she missed him, she knew he was happy and safe with her parents, their dog Cole, and their own cat, a Siamese named Bingo.

She'll see them all when she brought David home in a few days, if things continued to feel right outside of the resort, and with his family, wherever they were.

"Safe travels. We love you so much, Laurie," her mom said.

"Love you, too. See you sometime soon," Lauren replied, before disconnecting the call.

Elation tore through her as she jumped off of the bed and finished grabbing the rest of her stuff.

Lauren hadn't been gone five minutes when someone knocked on Joshua's door. Puzzled at how fast she had been, he opened the door with a grin. "Wow, that was quick —"

His words died in his throat when his gaze met his older brother Collin's. "What are you guys doing here?" He glanced to Collin's right and saw Jason, his middle sibling and twin to their sister, Angela. He took a step back, allowing them into the suite.

Closing the door behind them, he tightened the belt of his robe around his waist and leaned back against the door.

His brothers' faces were pale and solemn as they glanced at each other. Jason's brown eyes held a depth of sorrow, and there were worry lines around his mouth. Collin looked exhausted, and it seemed he had a few more grey hairs than he had when Joshua boarded the company jet heading for this tropical paradise.

Jason ran a hand through his short, black hair and cleared his throat. He glanced at Collin and nodded.

Joshua focused on his oldest brother, frustration rising in his chest. They were intruding on his time away from home and the family, and his time with Lauren. He wanted to be alone with her to tell her the truth about his name, his background and more without someone hovering, so he didn't have to hide his feelings for her.

He was falling for Lauren—faster than he dared dream about. He had loved Sybil, and she had felt the same, but it wasn't this intense, nor had it happened so fast or felt so right from the start. It had been a slow burn for them, building over the years until she was eighteen and he had finally asked her out, as a way to see if his feelings for his cousin's best friend were real or just something in passing, like most of his previous girlfriends had been. It had taken time, but he did fall for her eventually, and they had only been married a few short years before her untimely death.

With Lauren, it was an instant combustion, and felt real from the moment their gazes had met across ten feet of sand.

He wasn't going to let his brothers fuck this one up for him, like they had let that fucking twat Doyle almost fuck up Dana's life and steal her now defunct trust fund.

"What's the problem?" he demanded, his voice a bit sharper than what was tolerated around the family, and a lot ruder than he would have let out in public. Campbells didn't show their emotions outside of being coolly polite when out and about, even if they were grieving.

Until Sybil's death a year ago, he'd been able to play the game, only letting his public persona of a kind but distant man slip away when he was with Sybil and his cousins Dana, Ewan and their spouses.

At the moment, he had no patience for how a Campbell

man was *supposed to act*. He was annoyed as fuck and wanted both of his brothers out of his suite.

Collin shifted his feet on the carpet, the black designer shoes and dark grey suit looking out of place in a bright, cheerful spot like Sunrise Retreat. Jason scratched the back of his neck with his right hand, coughing into his left fist a few times.

"You need to pack," Collin said in his quiet baritone, the command in his voice evident. "We have to go home now."

Joshua's irritation grew. He was not going anywhere with them, especially not without Lauren. "Why should I? I have a few more days of relaxation left. I'm down here on your orders, Apisi," he growled, using his oldest brother's Siksika name.

His brothers looked at each other briefly, and Joshua could almost see the gears turning in their minds.

Finally, Jason let out a long breath and murmured, "It's Gramps."

Shock and worry zinged through him from head to toe. His and Jason's grandfather, their mother's father, was past eighty and wasn't in good health. "What about him?"

Collin pursed his lips and sighed. "I'm sorry brother, but he had a lot of pain last night. Gram and Uncle Murray took him to the emergency room."

Joshua stared at his oldest brother—half-brother actually—same father, different mothers—and nausea bubbled in his throat. "He's okay, right?"

A glance at Jason's pale face spoke volumes.

Collin shook his head, his dark eyes filled with sorrow. "I'm so sorry, Kitchi. Gramps didn't make it." Even though Collin wasn't related to Jason and Joshua's maternal grandparents—his mother had died when he was a toddler and their dad had married Yolanda a year later—he was considered a part of their family, too, and Joshua knew he loved Gram and

Gramps as much as the rest of them did.

His sorrow echoed in his voice, even though he was as cool and collected as ever. Jason was a bit more visibly shaken—his eyes were dull, and his hands trembled visibly as he clasped them together in front of his torso.

Joshua felt his knees giving way. He knew their mom's dad was on his way out, but hadn't been expecting it for a while, and especially not while he was on vacation, recovering from being a borderline alcoholic. He managed to get to the couch without falling, then flopped down on it hard.

Poor Gram, she must be in so much pain right now. Her pain at losing her husband of over sixty years must be crushing her. He choked out around the lump forming in his throat, "How's Gram doing?" It had just about killed him to lose Sybil, and they had only been married for a few years. Losing someone after spending that long together would be even more devastating.

Collin shrugged. "She's in shock and denial, like all of us are."

Joshua nodded. "When's the—" He couldn't say *funeral,* even a year after burying Sybil. Was he still that hung up on her, or was it his PTSD from finding her dead in their bathroom doing it?

He pushed the memory away and let out a long breath.

"You should go pack," Jason said quietly, grief evident in his voice, too, a lot stronger than Collin's had been. He and Gramps had spent a lot of time together, fishing and talking. Jason had been the closest to Gramps out of the four of them, so losing their mother's dad was probably hitting him like a million tons of bricks.

"Pack, yeah. I should." He stood and started heading toward the bedroom.

Pack . . . That's what he told Lauren to do. Go get her things so she could go home with him. He stopped short, whipped around and met Collin's gaze. "We can't go yet. Not until Lauren gets back."

The older men shared a puzzled glance. "Who's Lauren?"

Heat crept along his cheeks as he met his oldest brother's gaze. "Someone I met. I asked her to come home with me. She's in her room, packing, and will be here in a few minutes." He glanced at his watch, and noted it was twenty minutes since she had left, and just over fifteen minutes since his brothers had interrupted his oasis.

Collin's eyebrows shot up and a curious gleam appeared in his gaze. "You actually met someone you like that much in the short time you've been here?"

Jason blinked at him, his surprise sliding through his normally passive mask for a moment. "How can you have just met someone and want to bring her home to Grandfather? Isn't that too soon, and pretty presumptuous to bring her home without asking the family's permission?" There was a note of snark coloring the younger of his two brother's words, conveying that no one dared moved a muscle without their Grandfather Campbell's permission, let alone bring home someone they had just met to meet the family.

Irritation and anger sparked in Joshua's gut. Although he wanted to say where their grandfather could shove his attitude, he kept his voice even and calm as he replied, "Lauren is special. She's not like other women. She's beautiful, smart, funny, and witty."

"How so?" Jason demanded, the sarcasm in his voice getting stronger.

Collin held up a hand, always the peacemaker between the three of them. "I trust Josh's judgement," he stated quietly, his voice carrying a tonne of authority. "If he says she's a good person, we should give her a chance. *Right?*" He slid their brother a look with narrowed eyes.

Jason's lips thinned in annoyance, but he nodded. "We'll

meet her and see if she's good enough to meet the family," he muttered. With a long, hard look at first Collin, then Joshua, he said firmly, "If we find she isn't as wonderful as you say, I refuse to let her within twenty miles of the complex. Is that understood?"

Joshua let out a long sigh. Jason was the most rigid in following Grandfather Campbell's rules, no matter how stupid they seemed to the rest of the family. "You'll like her, Jace. I promise. She's great. She's a lot like your Madeline, but a lot louder." Jason's wife of twenty years was kind, gentle, and had a huge heart with a witty sense of humor, much like Lauren. He hoped that comparing Lauren to Madeline would soften Jason's view on things regarding bringing people home to the family, but didn't count on it.

Gentleness flickered through Jason's gaze for a second. He gave Joshua one last, hard stare before relaxing a smidgen. "If you say she is like Madeline, I'll be happy to meet her."

He couldn't help but grin at Jason, despite feeling sick about his maternal grandfather's death. "I'll go pack. If she shows up, come get me or send her back. She should be along at any minute."

"If she doesn't show up by the time you're done, we can go to her room to meet her. What floor is she on?" Collin said and pulled his phone out of his pocket.

Joshua's stomach dropped. He hadn't considered asking her what her room number was because she was supposed to be meeting him here, in his suite and staying until they left for Alberta in three days, together. He wasn't supposed to be dragged away by a family crisis. *Fucking hell.*

He glanced at his brothers and felt cold begin to penetrate his chest. "I'm not sure," he admitted in a mumble.

Collin blinked. "Well, we can find out by calling the front desk. What's her last name?"

Double fucking hell. The ice spread from his chest to his

stomach and started penetrating his limbs. "Uh . . . "

Collin blinked a few more times. "Where is she from? Do you know that much?"

Joshua shook his head, the chill claiming his head and moving into his head. Fuck, why hadn't he asked her any of this stuff?

A voice at the back of his mind told him that they were supposed to be telling each other everything, once she returned to his room, but she was nowhere in sight.

Jason glared at him. "You mean to tell us you were going to bring her home, and don't even know her last name? What the hell are you thinking?"

Collin shot Jason a filthy look. "Maybe they were too busy doing other things," he suggested and looked pointedly at Joshua.

He looked away, embarrassed that his brothers knew he had been too busy getting laid to ask his lover's last name—or much else about her.

Collin snorted and tapped a foot. "You have five minutes. Go pack. If she's not here by the time you're done, we can ask at the front desk about any Laurens staying at the resort."

Joshua ran into the bedroom, slamming the door behind him.

Where is she? Had she gotten cold feet about going to Alberta with him, and wasn't going to bother telling him?

His gut screamed its denial before the thought finished gelling in his head. She said she wanted to come home with him, but was something delaying her?

They had to wait another few minutes. His entire being screamed that if he didn't take her home with him, it was over, and he'd be forever lost.

Lauren was his salvation—his link back to the light.

He *could not*, and *would not* lose her.

Even if it cost him his family.

He took his time packing everything, delaying things as much as he could, but ten minutes was as long as his brothers were willing to give him.

Jason's sharp knock preceded him walking into the room. He glanced at the full suitcases standing at the ready and nodded at his youngest sibling with a cool gleam in his gaze. "It's time. We've waited too long for this woman to appear. She probably changed her mind."

Joshua didn't believe that any more than he believed the sun was going to rise in the west the following morning. He shot Jason a filthy look and glanced at his watch. Only half an hour had passed since his brothers had arrived. She should have been back to the suite over twenty minutes ago. *What was keeping her?*

"Come on, brother. Move. We have to get home as soon as possible. Grandfather wants us to return as soon as possible, so we can help Gram make arrangements for Gramps." Despite his obvious irritation that they were delayed, there was a note of pain in his tone.

Joshua sighed. "Please. Give her a little longer. She must have been held up by something. She promised me she'd be only a few minutes." They had to wait. It was either find her somehow or he may as well fade away to nothing. He needed her, desperately, and he didn't know how he was going to function without Lauren by his side, even after this short time.

Jason let out a long breath and his shoulders drooped. "I wish we could, but Collin is talking to Grandfather, who is wondering why we're not in the air yet. He's yelling a lot at Collin, and telling us to move it or lose it. We'd better go before he decides to start kicking ass and fires all of us." Sympathy coated his words, and although Joshua appreciated it, he still felt like their grandfather should fuck off and let Collin do his damn job.

Despite Collin taking over as official CEO of Campbell Incorporated, formerly Campbell Oil, a year ago, their meddling grandfather still called the shots, and was a tyrant if he didn't get his own way, despite being retired.

One more glance at his watch and Joshua ground his teeth together, feeling the iciness penetrate his entire being, including his heart and soul. His stomach rolled painfully as the knowledge that Lauren wasn't going to make it in time, and he was going to have to leave her behind, or his brothers will face their grandfather's wrath.

Slowly, he nodded, numbness echoing out of his motions. He lumbered toward Jason, feeling nausea rise in his throat.

Jason put a comforting hand on his shoulder and guided him out the door. "Let's go," he said to Collin, who nodded and opened the doors to the suite, where their men had been waiting.

"Get his suitcases. We'll be downstairs in the lobby when you're ready." Collin's voice sounded distant to Joshua's ears, and colder than it should have been.

Dully, he let his brothers lead him out of the suite where he and Lauren had pledged their commitment to each other, for the short term or the long, whatever awaited them. With a final glance at the sofa where they had made love, he turned away, determined to let her know what happened, somehow, somewhere along the way.

Reaching the lobby, Collin glanced at him. "We can ask about any Laurens staying here at the desk if you want to try getting a hold of her that way," he suggested, a warmth to his tone.

Relief ran through his entire soul as Joshua nodded. "Yeah. Let me talk to the clerk for a minute."

"We'll be leaving as soon as Lionel and Waylon finish packing your bags and bring the car around," Collin stated quietly with a hard clap on his shoulder.

Joshua nodded. It was so hard not to run to the desk and demand the clerk look up the names of every single woman staying at the resort that day. Instead, he took a deep breath and quietly walked over, noting no one was behind the counter. He hit the bell once, alerting the clerk, and prayed that somehow, he'd be able to get a message for her.

The same gentleman who had checked him in only five days ago appeared from around the corner with a smile, his name tag reading *Peter Malone, Front Desk Manager*. "Mr. Harper. Is there something I can do for you?" The fiftyish man with grey hair reminded him a lot of his Uncle Grayson, he had the same quiet and openly friendly demeanour.

"Actually, yes, I'd like to know if there's any single women with the first name of Lauren staying here." Heat flared along his ears and cheeks as he met the older man's blue gaze.

"Why, did you have a problem with someone?" Mr. Malone's eyes narrowed, and he moved to the computer holding all information about their guests. He started typing.

Joshua shook his head. "Um, no. I was hoping to find someone. She was supposed to meet me, but she's been delayed, and I can't wait any longer for her. I'm checking out. Family emergency." His stomach churned uncomfortably, and his hands were shaking.

Fuck, was he actually going to leave the resort without her as promised?

His entire soul screamed to *wait*—to see if she was really coming.

A glance at the elevators said otherwise. The only people he saw were families. No gorgeous redhead among them.

Mr. Malone nodded with a sly grin and typed in a few things. The computer beeped. "We have seven women named Lauren in the hotel right now. Do you know which floor she was staying on?"

Guiltily, he shook his head, and mumbled, "We didn't get that far. She was going to move into my room, until my brothers showed up. We waited for her, but there's no sign of her."

Mr. Malone frowned at the computer monitor for a moment as if he was considering something. "I could call each room to see if we can find her." He glanced at Joshua as if to confirm his suggestion.

"Do it. I don't care how long it takes. Please try them all." Relief had him sagging against the counter as he prayed she hadn't left her room yet if she had been delayed.

"One moment." Mr. Malone scooped up the phone receiver, typed in a number and waited. "Ah, yes. Is this Lauren? . . . I see. No, no problem, just doing a check to see if everything was okay . . . Fine. Thank you."

He hung up and glanced at Joshua. "That was the first one's wife."

One down, six to go. One in six wasn't bad odds, was it?

Mr. Malone dialed the next room on his list, pausing for a moment. "No answer." He hung up a moment later.

One down, one unsure. Joshua's stomach rolled again, a bit more painfully, like he had a sip of battery acid. What if that had been her room and she wasn't there?

"We will try again in a moment," the desk clerk said kindly, as if he had read Joshua's mind. He dialed another number, this time briskly saying, "Hello, this is the desk. We wanted to be sure everything was fine. Okay. Sorry to bother you." He hung up, and looked at Joshua. "That was her husband, the room is in her name."

Two down, one unsure. "Keep trying, and please hurry."

The desk clerk nodded and quickly made the calls. Out of the four remaining rooms, two were in and not the Lauren he was looking for, while the other two were not answering.

His gut screamed she had been in her room, or near it, at the time of the call. Which one of the three was anyone's guess.

Numbness inserted itself into his very being, and his entire body started shouting its denial. *Where the fuck was she?* Why didn't she answer the call? Did she really think so little of him that she decided to ditch him without saying a word?

Dizziness made him weave in place, and only a set of strong hands catching him saved him from embarrassing himself.

Collin's gentle command penetrated his brain. "Come on, brother. The car is here."

"No, not yet," Joshua said with a note of desperation. "We haven't gotten a hold of her. She could be on her way to my room now." He turned and glared at his oldest sibling, who was staring at him intently.

Collin sighed. "The jet is in its pre-flight mode right now. We're leaving in less than twenty minutes. Grandfather's orders." His eyes carried a mountain of sympathy, but he looked determined to follow protocol even if it killed his baby brother. He glanced at the desk and back to meet Joshua's glower. "Leave a note for her." He motioned to Mr. Malone.

"We need some paper and a pen, fast," Collin stated, giving the command as he always did, with kindness and making it seem like a request instead.

Two seconds later, a notepad with the *Sunrise Retreat* header on it and a matching pen were pushed in front of them on the desk. Joshua grabbed the pen, and scribbled a quick note to Lauren, while Collin stood by, his hand on Joshua's shoulder as if to give him a measure of support.

Out of his siblings, only Collin seemed to get the agony of being separated from the ones he loved most, and it seemed his brother understood how hard it was to leave Lauren behind.

He quickly read the note over to be sure he conveyed everything he wanted to tell her in a few short lines.

Lauren,

I'm so sorry I had to disappear on you, but my brothers arrived with some horrible news. My grandfather died this morning, and we have to go home right away. We waited as long as we could, but had to leave without you due to our flight.

I'm so sorry we missed you. Call me at the number below, and I'll send a plane for you, so you can visit my family as I promised.

I miss you so much already.

Love, Joshua Davidson Campbell

With a long sigh, he folded the paper in half and slid it into the envelope Mr. Malone had provided for him. He scrawled *Lauren* on the front of it and sealed it, placing a kiss on his finger and sliding it along her name before handing it to the clerk.

"She's the one with red hair, and blue eyes," he reminded the gentleman.

Malone nodded with a sympathetic smile. "I remember her. She's very pleasant, always chatting about how lovely it is here, and how much she's enjoying everything." He tapped the envelope with the precious letter in it on the counter twice. "I'll give it to her myself."

Gratitude dulled his agony of being ripped away from Lauren for a split second. "Thank you, and thank you for your kindness."

"You're welcome, Mr. Harper. You're welcome here any time. Have a safe trip home, and I'm sorry about the family emergency." He reached out a hand, and Joshua shook it. Collin did the same.

"Thank you," Joshua replied.

As Collin guided him toward the door, he couldn't help but take one long, last look toward the elevators and the stairs, looking for her.

When no sign of her glorious crimson hair appeared, Joshua swallowed back a sob, and felt his entire body go numb.

She isn't going home with me, after all.

Chapter Ten

L auren had just exited her suite when the phone inside be-gan to chime. With a few choice swear words, she quickly unlocked the door again, leaving her bags in the hall and making a dive for the ringing annoyance.

A dead line echoed in her ear when she lifted the receiver.

Whoever it was must have hung up. She put the receiver back into its cradle and hummed a tune as she exited the suite again, this time lingering to be sure no one else tried calling that room.

She hadn't meant to talk to her mom for more than twenty minutes, then having to put up with her dad's call so he could bawl her out for being so impulsive. It was times like that when she wished she had another sister, so maybe her parents wouldn't go off the deep end each time she did something that wasn't within her normal behavior. That was another ten-minute delay.

She was over eighteen and lived in her own apartment, for fuck's sake. She had a life and could make decisions for herself even if she was working for the family business.

Two minutes later, she and her bags were in the elevator, going up to David's floor. Excitement rose in her chest as she recalled the gentleness and affection in his gaze before she zipped downstairs.

She glanced at her watch, annoyed that her family had taken up over half an hour of the time she could have been in bed or having a bath with David, making love, or just talking.

There would be plenty of time for that later, she reminded

herself when the elevator dinged and she glanced upwards. Joy zinged through her body as she saw it was his floor.

Finally, she was going to be with the man who had made her soul sing with delight, and who had given her the most intense and amazing orgasms of her life.

She grabbed her bags, lifting one and pulling the other behind her as she exited the lift, and sauntered toward his room.

Something felt off as she turned the corner. It seemed too bright around his doorway. Had he left the room door open or was he hurt?

She turned the corner, saw the open door and noted the cleaning cart in the hall.

Housecleaning. That made perfect sense as to why the room was open.

With a smile, she poked her head in and called, "David? Are you here?"

A few footsteps thudded in the back, toward the bedroom. A thin, tall woman about her own age with white skin, blue eyes and brown hair, wearing a uniform appeared. "Can I help you?"

Lauren smiled at the woman. "I'm looking for the man who is staying in this room."

The worker frowned, her eyes blinking repeatedly. "The room is empty. We're in the middle of cleaning it for the next guests."

Empty? "What? There was someone staying here. A man. He was tall and has long, black hair." She hadn't got the wrong room, had she?

A glance at the door showed the correct suite number, 805.

The woman walked a few steps closer. "There was a gentleman in here, but he left a few minutes ago. His brothers came and got him. Family emergency."

Brothers? David has brothers?

Her eyes went wide as it sank in that he had checked out, and hadn't waited for her to arrive. *Fucking hell!* She eyed the worker again, and demanded, "How long ago did he leave?" Her stomach started sinking, fast. Why didn't he wait for her?

The woman shrugged. "He left his bags, so we had to wait until someone came for them." She glanced at the clock. "They left five minutes ago, right after he did."

She had missed him by only a few minutes! Elation zinged through her as she grabbed the handles of her fallen bags. "Thank you! You've been a huge help."

Lauren turned, and barely got around the corner in her haste to reach the elevators.

Seeing the numbers in the high twenties on both as she came near them, she prepared herself for a long eight story trip down the stairs.

"Please, let him still be in the lobby, or on the elevators going down." She went down the stairs as fast as her heels and her suitcases would let her.

Five minutes later, she thudded against the door to the lobby, her breath coming in gasps in her rush to catch David before he left. Cursing her inability to shut up with her mother or refuse to listen to her father ranting, she hoped she wasn't too late to catch him before he left.

She pushed the door to the lobby open and looked around. People milled about, sitting in chairs, talking, reading books or the local news, watching TV or just relaxing in the two sitting areas of the foyer, not far from the desk.

None of them were tall, with long black hair and a smile that could melt her soul in seconds.

Pulling her bag behind her and sucking in air, she navigated her way to the desk, where a young woman with dark eyes and blond hair sat, typing and glancing through papers from time to time.

"Excuse me, but did you see a man with long, black hair lately?" she asked the woman.

The lady shook her head. "I'm sorry, but no, I haven't. I came on a few minutes ago, to cover while Peter is helping the Harpers load their things into their limo."

A glance out the door showed the desk manager shaking hands with a tall man who had his back to her. They clapped each other on the shoulder and the man with dark hair climbed into the black limousine and shut the door.

Something about that man felt familiar, like she had seen him before . . .

Lauren tried seeing through the windows of the car as it passed by the lobby windows, but the windows were tinted, and the sun was shining into the lobby, creating a glare.

She ran out of the hotel door, looked around and felt her stomach collide with the soles of her feet. David was nowhere to be seen, and it appeared that Mr. Malone, the desk manager, had vanished as well.

Her recollection hit on the man who had gotten into the car. She hadn't gotten a good look at him, other than to notice his face was tanned, he was well dressed, and he had black hair, and wore a dark, solemn suit.

Her memory betrayed her again as the recollection of the other man came into view.

"*No*," she hissed, and without thinking, ran in the same direction the car had gone, her heels slowing her down.

She kicked them off, felt the heat of the pavement and gravel beneath her bare soles as she ran, what felt like for her life.

Skidding to a stop at the end of the long driveway, and looking out around the trees, she found the entire road deserted. The only thing moving was the tree branches, the only sounds the rustling of the wind in the trees, her own breathing as she gasped for air, and the hurried beating of her now-broken heart.

Lauren collapsed, her bum hitting the gravel, her shock at

missing David by only a minute slapping her mind.

Her stunned silence broke after a moment, and a keening wail echoed around the entrance to the resort.

CHAPTER ELEVEN

Joshua's House, Campbell Complex
Langdon, Alberta, Canada

Gramps' funeral passed in a numbing blur. Joshua vaguely remembered the mourners, his mother and grandmother's tears and his siblings and cousins on the Eaglewind side of his family looking dazed as he felt.

That night, he spent the first night in his house alone since the day before his Cousin Dana's wedding. The silence of the house penetrated his brain, screaming at him from every wall, every corner, and every miniscule dot seemed to mock him. The darkness invaded his mind, pushing the light that had gathered there after going to Nova Scotia and starting his journey toward being sober, the light that had brightened after he met her.

Lauren . . .

Just thinking her name sent shockwaves of agony through every nerve ending, his heart, his brain and his soul.

Why didn't his fucking grandfather let them wait another ten minutes? He was sure if they had delayed their departure from the hotel even another minute or so, she would have found him and been there with him at that moment.

He *needed* her. She was essential to his well-being, his sanity, his very *survival*.

He didn't know her last name, or where she was from. How was he going to find her?

Why didn't he tell her his real name so she could have

found him? Or at least get her last name so he could have found her, somehow?

The questions burned into his mind for days upon days, and he slowly spiraled back down into another deep depression, unable to leave the house, and in two weeks, he barely left his bed.

He couldn't eat, couldn't sleep, and couldn't go near the room he'd stayed in with Sybil.

He had lost the two women who had made him whole—first Sybil, and now Lauren.

Sybil's death was no one's fault—he'd had that drilled into his head by Ewan and Marti, Dana and Avery, and his brothers—but the guilt had resurfaced, making him wonder if he had taken her to the hospital, would she still be alive, and so many more *what ifs*.

Anger slowly invaded his mind as he recalled how inhumane his grandfather had been with Avery, Dana's husband. The old man had tried forbidding her to marry Avery, all because he was assigned female at birth, not male, and how he had changed his body to reflect on his true gender, and more. Joshua blamed the old man for splitting the family apart, despite Dana's parents defying his grandfather like his Uncle Grayson and Aunt Abby had.

The rage slowly ate its way into hate, and having his grandfather show up at his door was the final straw.

It was a month after the funeral and being ripped away from Lauren, and a week since Joshua started staying in bed all day, not eating, barely moving except to go to the bathroom and drinking a bit of water. He felt constantly ill, and he could feel his mind slipping back to the way things were in the year after Sybil's death, before he met Lauren.

The doorbell rang several times. He ignored it, burying himself deeper into the covers, just wanting to hide. Not even a snowstorm could stop a determined Campbell. He'd learned that the hard way several years ago, while he was still living with his parents, and his Uncle Darren had arrived on skis.

The snowstorm raging outdoors wasn't stopping whoever it was banging on his door that day. It could have been what triggered the initial blast, that or his grandfather's attitude. Joshua wasn't sure what made him explode, but it was the day he realized family was not everything—especially now.

He crawled out of his nest and stumbled toward the front door from the spare room, the one he and Sybil had planned to turn into a nursery. It hadn't been started yet, but a brand-new crib sat in its box, unassembled in the corner, and a rock-ing chair was already by the window, silently waiting for the child that was never conceived.

Dizzily, he grabbed the doorknob, unlocked the deadbolt and stared at the person who dared to invade his grief and anger.

"You look like hell, boy. Did you just get out of bed?" his grandfather demanded sharply. His long white hair was cov-ered by a toque, and a black parka covered him from shoulder to knees.

A glance outside showed the weather had turned sunny in the last few hours since Joshua looked out the window. Or was that days? Time was blurring together for him. He barely knew or cared if it was day or night, or if it was cold or warm. He only knew about the snowstorm because of the wind the other day. Or was that yesterday?

A headache pounded at the back of his head, in his ears and into his throat. "What do you want?" he asked in greet-ing, ignoring the old man's question.

Viktor's eyebrows shot up, and a cold glare spread into his brown gaze before he glanced down at Joshua's shorts and bare legs in disgust. "You're supposed to greet guests fully dressed," he scolded with a snort.

Irritation crawled up Joshua's spine. "You're not a guest. I didn't invite you," he muttered, but stepped back to allow his grandfather into his house.

Grandfather's gaze darkened as he looked around the kitchen.

Shame zipped through Joshua's brain as he realized how filthy the house was. Dirty dishes, left over from the funeral, were piled up beside the sink, glasses were all over the table, and a full ashtray was by the stove. He hadn't bothered to toss that out once he had started his quitting journey, having stayed with Ewan in Nova Scotia during the first two months of his journey to break his alcoholism. He felt his ears and cheeks burning as the old man scrutinized the mess, his lips compressing into a deep frown and his eyes shooting daggers at Joshua.

"What the fuck are you doing, wallowing in filth? This place is disgusting, and it smells!" Grandfather snapped, his dark eyes flashing disdain and horror. He came a step closer and took a huge sniff. "Ugh, it's not the house I smell, it's you!" he bellowed.

Humiliation tingled every single one of Joshua's nerve endings. This was *his* house. The old man had arrived without an invitation or without warning. Had he known, he would have at least had a shower and tried cleaning up a bit. He and Sybil didn't like servants in their private area, preferring to do it all themselves.

Unfortunately, his depression had taken over, and having no word from Lauren had only made him feel worse. Knowing she hadn't reached out to him like he had hoped said it all. She didn't want to explore a future with him, as she had said, and the knowledge it was over kept ringing through his mind, spiralling him deeper and deeper into sorrow.

He opened his mouth to apologize, but Viktor cut him off

with a wave of his hand. "Get your ass in the shower, and get cleaned up while I call someone in to clean up this pigsty!" he bellowed, and slammed the side of his fist on top of the counter, creating a huge crack and shaking it so badly that a plate fell off the pile beside the sink and crashed to the floor, shattering.

That snapped Joshua out of his daze. He stared at the shards of the plate, one of the set given to him and Sybil on their wedding day by her parents. The numbness and grief evaporated from his mind like a blown light bulb.

"Are you deaf?" Grandfather hissed. "I told you to move!" He cracked his cane against the refrigerator door, the sound reverberating in his mind.

"No," Joshua muttered, shaking his head. The fog was slowly lifting, but his grandfather's words when he'd arrived home began echoing in his mind.

Don't you have anything to do, other than stare out the window, boy? Your family needs you here, not somewhere else, with god knows who . . .

With god knows who . . . with god knows who . . . with god knows who . . .

Another loud crack echoed in his ears, this time from grandfather hitting a chair with his cane, and bellowing, "I said move, boy! Now!" He lifted his cane and took a step toward Joshua.

With a loud, primal yell, Joshua felt the anger of the last eighteen months finally break free, and Joshua grabbed the walking stick aimed at his head.

"Stop it!" he screamed, pushing at the cane and glaring at the man who had caused so much trouble for him, his siblings, and his cousins—so much trouble that Ewan and Dana had moved away, and that his own brother Collin wasn't able to do a damn thing with a company he was supposed to be running. "Get the fuck out of my house!" Joshua yelled, slamming his own fist on the counter, taking a slow, threatening step toward the old geezer who wouldn't leave him or anyone else in the family alone in peace.

His grandfather's eyes were wide in shock for a split second, before narrowing into a glare. "What did you just say, boy?" His voice was low, cold and measured, an indication of severe consequences if his orders were not followed to the letter.

Joshua's grief over losing the one person who could help him find the light in his darkness rose to the surface and burst out in the largest explosion to ever erupt from his temper.

One second he was opening his mouth to tell his grandfather to go fuck himself, the next he felt his fist connecting with bone and muscle. "Get out of my fucking house, you old prick!" he screamed, and jumped at the old man.

An extra dose of rage fueling his motions, he shoved his grandfather to the floor and landed on top of him. His hands locked around Viktor's throat, feeling the geezer's windpipe close as his fingers tightened, screaming, "I hate your fucking guts, you old bastard! You made me give up the one person who could bring me joy, you fucking selfish piece of shit!"

A set of hands grabbed him, pulling him off of his stunned grandfather, but his rage was so severe, he broke free and lunged for the old man once more.

"Joshua, *stop*!" someone yelled as he fisted his hand, ready to punch his grandfather into oblivion. "Come on, man! I think he got your message!"

"Get Father out to the car," someone ordered. It sounded like one of his uncles, Darren.

Joshua fought against the people holding him back and bellowed his hate for the one person who seemed to enjoy hurting others, especially his own family. "Never ever come back, you fucking old jackass, you hear me?" he screamed. "I hate you and every fucking thing you've done to me! I hope you fucking die alone, you old bastard!"

He managed to get a step in before someone else hauled him back.

"Tanya, get Uncle Grayson, and Aunt Abby, now! We need help in here."

A door slamming snapped him out of his rage, and he shook his head.

"Easy, man. Calm down. The old man is gone." Symon's voice registered in Joshua's mind.

Dully, he tried standing on his own, but dizziness overcame him. He started sliding to the floor, but someone caught him. He turned his head to blink at his cousin-in-law.

The other man's blue eyes were wide with concern, and a soft frown was on his face. "Jesus, man. You okay?"

Symon's gentle inquiry about his health and well-being made Joshua's anger evaporate, and numbness settled in again.

He nodded and cleared his throat. "I think so. I haven't eaten yet, that's probably why I'm not feeling the greatest," he mumbled.

Symon gave him a knowing look, his normally pale skin a bit pinkish around his cheekbones. "Is that why you knocked out the old man?"

Shock zinged through his system before the numbness and cold returned, faster than it had before. He shook his head. "He pissed me off and tried hitting me."

Symon nodded once and let out a long sigh. "I saw that. Fucking old jerk, he's getting worse as the years go on."

"Yeah," Joshua replied with a sarcastic smile, letting it fade. He shook off his cousin-in-law's hand and stumbled to a chair, managing to land on it without falling over.

Symon flopped down on the wooden chair next to his. "Fucking old coot. Tanya, Darren, Grayson and I told him to leave you alone and we'd take care of you, but he wouldn't listen. He had to barge his way in before we were out the door of the mansion. He snuck out before we could stop him." He stood up, went to the fridge and got an ice pack.

He dropped it on the table between the coffee mugs and the filthy glasses, motioning to Joshua to put it on his hand.

Joshua glanced down, noting his knuckles were scuffed and swelling. He might have hit the floor a few times while trying to strangle the old man—that must be why his hand was puffing up and starting to hurt.

It was tempting to let it go and let the agony fuel more anger, but he was so tired, and as Symon had told him, he'd gotten his point across. He complied and shivered when the cold hit his injured skin.

"Tan called a few of the maids that work at her parents' place. They'll be here shortly to help you clean up, unless you want a shower first." Symon's gentle words penetrated Joshua's brain, making him look up.

"No one has to help me. I can do it myself," he mumbled, glancing around at the disaster in the kitchen. Shame burned along every nerve ending again, but it wasn't a hurtful shame. It was the guilty kind, like he had forgotten to do something.

"Hey, no worries. Tan and I don't mind helping. Neither do your aunt and uncle, especially if they get the kids for a few hours, ya know?" Symon grinned, his eyes sparkling.

Joshua snickered at his friend slash cousin-in-law's remark. Darren and Bertha were proud grandparents several times over and loved babysitting their grandchildren. Tanya and Symon had two girls, and had hoped for more, but hadn't had any luck.

"Yeah, I know," he replied, the left side of his mouth lifting a little.

Symon reached over and clapped him on the shoulder. "Go on, have a shower. We'll get things straightened up. Grayson and Levi will handle the old man."

Joshua shrugged. "I don't give a fuck what the old asshole

does to me. He's already ruined my life and chased away the two cousins who are the other two parts of me. What he does to me now has no meaning. I'm beyond caring." He stood, weaving in place for a moment before getting his bearings.

Symon's eyes darkened. "Don't say that. He can make your life a hell of a lot worse. He could kick you out of the family like he did to Dana."

Memories of how awful Dana had been treated a year ago by the old coot rose in Joshua's mind, setting an ember smouldering once more. He inhaled deeply and let it out slowly.

The old prick knew how he felt and how deeply his hate went. With some luck, he'd have peace, unless the fucking dickhead he called grandfather decided he needed to be taught another lesson, which was possible.

Ah well—like he had said to his cousin-in-law, nothing the old man did to him mattered. As far as he was concerned, death would be welcomed at this point, just to get him out of the hell he had been in since Lauren abandoned him a few weeks earlier.

He wove his way into the hall, making sure Symon didn't follow.

He needed a drink, a big one, and he knew exactly where to find a bottle.

With a scoff of disgust, Joshua walked into the bathroom, lifted the cover of the toilet tank, scooped out a bottle of whiskey and cracked it open.

To hell with the family, and to hell with everything else. He was dead inside and would never be alive again.

Raising the bottle to his lips, he opened his mouth and felt the burn of alcohol slide down his throat.

Lauren's Apartment
That same night . . .

The double lines on the stick she held in her hand blurred as Lauren gasped in shock. Three tests, all with the same results.

Positive.

No, it couldn't be true. She was *not* pregnant. They had been so careful. Even during that one unprotected time in the water, he had pulled out and ejaculated into the water.

Besides, the pill was supposed to be effective, right?

A tingle at the back of her mind reminded her that even though the pill was a reliable type of contraception, it could be fallible sometimes.

Her arm went limp, and her hand dangled between her knees, losing its grip on the pregnancy test.

Marmalade, now almost fully grown, wound his way around between her legs, purring and rubbing his face against her hand.

She let out a long sigh, feeling grief and agony welling in her chest. Her eyes closed, and tears burned her lids.

With a loud whimper, she slid to the floor, lying in a puddle on the bathmat, then started sobbing her grief over not being able to find her unborn child's father and how he'd abandoned her without a word.

"David, where are you?" she whimpered. "Please, please find me. I need you. We need you!" she cried into the silence of her lonely home. The only thing answering her was the purring of her beloved cat and the wind echoing in the trees beside her window.

With a soft sob, she pulled Marmalade into her arms and cried for herself and the unborn child that would never know its father.

To Be Continued . . .

ABOUT THE AUTHOR

Sexy Romance, Nova Scotia style.

V.J. Allison was born and raised in southern Nova Scotia, Canada, and her work reflects her strong Maritime roots. She is a stay-at-home mother to a son on the autism spectrum, married to the love of her life, and "mama" to a rescued Maine Coon cat named Marnie. She has been writing various stories of novel length and short stories since her school days and sees writing as a vital component to her life.

She is a small town erotic romance author published by Extasy Books, and her novels have been received with great acclaim. Two of her novels, *Away to Me* and *Honestly,* are recipients of the Extasy Books ***Editor's Choice Seal of Excellence and Enjoyable Reading***.

When she isn't writing, she loves to read romance and science fiction novels (notably *Star Wars*); listen to music (heavy metal, rock, alternative); and do graphics design. She runs her own graphics design company, *V.J. Allison Art*, specializing in t-shirt and other merchandise designs, along with book covers and other custom graphic arts. She is also an editor, and spends a lot of time helping other authors.

This self-proclaimed geeky rocker chick is a warrior and advocate for various chronic illnesses including Occipital Neuralgia, Trigeminal Neuralgia, Diabetes, Migraines, and Glossopharyngeal Neuralgia. She is also an advocate for the prevention of animal cruelty and is a voice for marginalized communities.

Find her books at https://books2read.com/ap/8Z2M90/VJ-Allison